THE BODY IN THE CAR PARK

More crimes for Casey Clunes to solve. A body is found in a multi-storey car park, and by the sound of it, the deceased has antagonised any number of people . . . When a horse bolts at the local riding stables, and the body of a young girl is found, it looks like an unfortunate accident. But soon, further information comes to light . . . And in standalone story, *Deadline News*, D.I. Ed Bailey finds himself investigating a crime which hits close to home.

GERALDINE RYAN

◆

THE BODY IN THE CAR PARK
& OTHER STORIES

Complete and Unabridged

LINFORD
Leicester

First published in Great Britain

First Linford Edition
published 2018

A catalogue record for this book is available
from the British Library.

ISBN 978–1–4448–3601–1

Published by
F. A. Thorpe (Publishing)
Anstey, Leicestershire

Set by Words & Graphics Ltd.
Anstey, Leicestershire
Printed and bound in Great Britain by
T. J. International Ltd., Padstow, Cornwall

This book is printed on acid-free paper

The Body in the Car Park

Casey fished out Finlay's lunch box from the bottom of his schoolbag and sighed. It was always the same. Unless someone reminded her son to remove it the night before so it could be washed up ready for next day, it would inevitably remain languishing at the bottom of his bag overnight.

Of course, by 'someone', she meant Dom. He'd been on Daddy Duty last night while she'd been on that child witness questioning course. *She* never forgot when it was her turn to take the domestic helm. Just like she never forgot to remove the washing from the machine or put the bins out for the refuse collection. But then, she was a woman, capable of multi-tasking and, as Dom was forever reminding her, pretty damned-near perfect.

'Finlay! We're walking today, remember? Mummy's car's in the garage. So we need to leave in ten minutes.'

Finlay appeared at the top of the stairs, clothed in his neat navy and grey school uniform, but barefoot.

'I can't find any socks that match, Mummy,' he said, plaintively, just as Casey's phone started ringing. 'I think the washing machine's swallowed them up again.'

'I'll be up in a second, sweetheart,' she replied. 'I just need to get the phone in case it's work.'

It wasn't work at all. It was their new neighbour, Euan. He sounded desperate.

'Casey,' he said, 'Michelle's gone into labour. I'm going to have to take her into hospital, right now.'

'But the baby isn't due for another three weeks!'

'I know. Little blighter obviously didn't get the memo.'

Casey smiled.

'Thing is, Michelle's mum can't get here until this evening and we wondered if . . . ?'

'Ella. I can take her to school, and Dom can pick her up and keep her here

4

until Michelle's mum arrives.' Casey was happy to help.

Finlay's sharp ears must have picked up Ella's name. He came bounding down the stairs and into the kitchen. Not only had he found his socks, he'd put them on, along with his shoes. He appeared to have dragged a comb through his dark locks too. Could this be love? she wondered.

'Well, looks like Finlay's ready to go,' she said, directing her words to Euan. 'We'll pop round and collect Ella right away. She doesn't mind walking, I hope?'

There was a tense silence.

'Is there a problem, Euan?'

'Um . . . Thing is, Casey, she's still in her pyjamas. Our routine seems to have gone to pot somewhat this morning.'

'Well, it's not every day a new baby decides to make an appearance.'

Casey racked her brains. They could do what she'd planned and walk anyway — given the circumstances, school would surely understand. But the Super would be less than forgiving if she arrived half an hour late for the daily briefing.

'It's not a problem,' she said. 'One more won't make any difference. I'll take Dom's car since it's sitting out front and his keys are here.'

'Thanks, Casey,' Euan said. 'You've saved the day.'

*   *   *

'You excited about getting a new baby brother or sister, Ella?'

Casey peered through her rear view mirror as they chugged down the road, stopping and starting every ten seconds due to the traffic lights. Dom's car was a disgrace — sweet wrappers and discarded newspapers everywhere. Not to mention his smelly kit from last night's gym session. More terrifying, though, was the funny rattling sound coming from the engine.

Ella turned her massive chocolate-brown eyes towards Casey and gave a barely perceptible nod. She sat there in the back seat, hugging Patch — the black and white toy dog she took with her everywhere — close to her chest.

'Why can't we have a new baby?' Finlay piped up.

Casey was taken aback by this sudden, unexpected question. 'That's a big decision, Finlay. Not one I can make on my own.'

'That's what Daddy said. He said he'd need to have a discussion with you about it,' replied Finlay.

So Finlay had asked Dom too? Dom certainly hadn't mentioned it to her.

'So why don't you have it, then? Tonight. When I've gone to bed.'

Casey grinned at him. Finlay would be brilliant down the station in the interview room. Once he got the bit between his teeth, he refused to let go. A new baby, though. Both she and Dom had been only children, and even as grown-ups were prone to wondering if they'd missed out.

But she'd be forty in a couple of weeks. And Dom was four years older. She was just in the middle of making a list of disadvantages to having a second child, when she noticed the unmistakable, acrid smell of smoke. There it was — wafting across the back window, at first a wisp, then a tongue, but very soon a fog.

There was nothing else for it. She had to get the kids out, quickly and without alarming them.

'Right, kids,' she said, 'change of plan. We're walking the rest of the way. Finlay, undo your belt. Ella, I'm coming to get you.'

'Okay, Mum,' Finlay said, seemingly unaware of any danger.

Fumbling with Ella's seatbelt, she accidentally knocked Patch the dog onto the floor. Ignoring it, she swiftly pulled the little girl out. Finlay, who'd managed to unbuckle his seat belt himself, was out in a jiff. Casey's relief that the danger was over was short-lived, however. No sooner had she shepherded the children to the bus shelter for safety than Ella set up a wail.

'Patch! I have to go back inside and get him!'

'No! That's impossible.'

Ella was too quick for her. The little girl slipped her grasp, ran towards the car and clambered back inside. Casey was frozen to the spot. Then, from the corner of her eye, she glimpsed the shadowy figure of a young man hurtling towards the car. She watched, horrified, as he disappeared into the smoking interior, reappearing almost immediately, pulling Ella — holding tight to her beloved Patch — behind him.

'Get right away,' the stranger said, pushing Ella towards her. 'All of you. It could blow up any second.'

What Casey really wanted to do, now Ella was in her arms, was hug her tight. But she was a professional. This was no time to go to pieces. Pulling herself together she made a call to the Fire Service, before warning the huddle of passers-by, drawn to the scene by all the excitement, to cross over the road. Seconds later there was a loud explosion and Dom's car was in flames.

The fire brigade was at the scene in no time. When the fire was finally out and the onlookers began to drift away, Casey turned this way and that to look for their rescuer. But there was no sign of him. He seemed to have disappeared into thin air.

* * *

For a man who needed to remain under the radar, Stefan had behaved in a way that was designed to draw attention. Everyone took pictures these days. What if his image had been captured by some bystander?

That woman with the children — she was a mother. She'd be bound to talk about what happened with her husband; maybe even go to the police. He could see it now. *This man saved my little girl. I'd like to reward him but I don't know where to find him.* Step forward the amateur photographer, a member of the great British public, ready and willing to do their bit for a happy ending.

Except it wouldn't be a happy ending. Before he knew it, his face would be plastered all over the local news. Brockhaven was a small town. They'd find him in no time. And how long would it be before the gratitude and applause died down and suspicion and questions took their place? What would happen to him then? And not just him, but to his brother, too.

'Why can't you mind your own

business?' Nicu had yelled at him. What could he say? You're my big brother. I love you. I only want to help. What would he do now, when this morning's news got back to him?

He should have listened when Nicu told him to keep out of his affairs. 'The trouble with you is, you're always sticking your nose in. This is England, not Romania.'

He knew that. Of course he did. But England was the home of cricket, wasn't it? The game where everyone played fair. He hadn't played fair, this Jay Brennan, his brother's boss. He needed to be told. All Stefan had done was to pay him a visit and try to reason with him. But that man knew nothing about reason. So he'd had to stick up for his brother by other means . . .

★   ★   ★

In the end, Casey was only thirty minutes late for the daily briefing. She could have been later — what with having to wait for someone to turn up and scrape the

11

remains of Dom's poor car off the road, and for the police too, who, she was informed, would need to take a statement.

Thankfully, P.C.s Tommy Hunter and Beth Tranter were on the scene in no time. And more thankfully, they volunteered not only to drive Casey to the school to drop off her charges, but to run her straight on to the station.

En route they filled her in about a new investigation. The body of a man had been found the previous afternoon, in his car, on the top floor of the multi-storey car park. He hadn't yet been identified, and it was still unclear if anyone else had been involved. The car had been badly keyed though, which suggested someone had possibly held a grudge against the driver.

Typical, Casey thought. If she hadn't been on that course she could have been first on the scene. She was almost tempted to ask Tommy to put the blue light on so they could get to the station a bit faster, but wondered if maybe the residents of Brockhaven High Street had

had enough excitement for one morning already.

The Super glanced at his watch in a very unsubtle manner as Casey strode in and took a seat. She could have told him exactly why she was late, but she was as keen as he was to get down to business. She'd heard about the body in the car park, she said, taking a seat. He nodded in the direction of D.C. Jody Bright, who, he said, had just had some new information.

Jody, keen as mustard to impress as ever, sat up straight, adjusted her collar and began.

'Jay Brennan, thirty-five years old. Identified this morning by one of his staff. Runs a club out Devden way. The Night Flower, it's called.'

'I know him,' Casey said. 'We picked up a couple of kids with false IDs on them and they were daft enough to tell us which club had let them in. So I paid him a visit. Couple of months ago, now.'

Brennan had put his hands up right away and accepted a caution. Their exchange had been over and done with in no time.

'Did you form any opinion of him?' the Super asked.

'Wasn't in his company long enough,' Casey replied. 'He told me he was new to the post and that he was turning the place round, getting rid of old staff who'd been a bit too lax, and hiring new ones he could be sure were on the same page he was. He said he was after the over-25s market,' she said. 'Wanted to smarten the place up.'

When somebody muttered that it needed it, there were nods of agreement all round. You could be wading knee deep in vomit some Friday nights, according to one of the uniformed officers at the table.

'I don't suppose there's been a PM done on him yet?' Casey directed her question at Jody.

Jody shook her head. 'Not yet,' she said. 'We'll know more later.'

Casey nodded. 'Witnesses? Statements?'

'Too early,' Jody said. 'Uniform are in the process of checking the system at the car park. Shouldn't take too long, it was a

Monday afternoon. If it had been a Saturday, the place would've been rammed. But there wouldn't have been that many cars parked there at that time.'

There was a knock at the door and Gail Carter came in, smart in her new sergeant's uniform. She shot Casey a look of concern.

'I didn't think you'd be in,' she said. 'I heard about your accident.'

Casey grimaced, as if to say that what had happened had been nothing to get excited about.

'What accident?' The Super was suddenly intrigued.

'Just a spot of bother,' Casey muttered, shooting Gail a look that said 'not a word'.

Always good at taking a hint, Gail switched subjects. 'I've got the CCTV from the car park. We may have a suspect.'

The atmosphere in the room changed abruptly from lethargic to anticipatory. Gail handed the tape to one of the junior officers who deftly installed it in the machine, while Jody Bright shot out of her seat and quickly closed the blinds.

The tape started up, blurred and grainy, cutting from the lift doors to the stairwells with short, irritating clicks.

'This is the bit you might be interested in,' Gail said. 'Here. Look.'

The tape froze as the ground floor exit door of the multi-storey opened to reveal, just for a second, the figure of a man; small, slim, with dark features. His expression was grim, determined. He was dressed in the ubiquitous uniform of hoody and jeans. He could have been any young man in his early twenties. Yet something was niggling her, tugging at her memory.

'Go back,' she said.

'How far?'

'Stop. Now go forward.'

There it was. The flat palm on the sticky glass door. What was it she'd seen? Yes, of course. There on his left wrist. A leather surfer bracelet. The image was black and white, but she knew that the darker colour on the bracelet was, in fact, a brilliant red. Because she'd seen it earlier. On the wrist of the guy who'd

16

pulled Ella out of the car and fled before she could turn to thank him.

★ ★ ★

It had been Casey's idea to put together an identikit picture of the man on the CCTV tape she believed could be the same one who'd rescued Ella from the car. Gail, who was much more familiar with the composite faces programme than she was herself, clicked her way through what seemed like hundreds of examples of facial features, until she finally arrived at a version of the face that Casey remembered.

Meanwhile, forensics had come through to say that the lacerations to the back of the head were proof enough to suspect foul play. As for the keying, that could have been done on another occasion, it was impossible to tell. Currently, the car park was designated a crime scene and officers were in the process of contacting the owner of every car that had been parked there at any time on the day of the murder, up until

14.30, the time the body was found. The victim's car had been towed away for further investigation.

Jody had been right in her estimation that the car park would have been pretty much unoccupied on a Monday. In fact, fewer than one hundred vehicles had used it between seven a.m. and when Jay Brennan's body had been discovered. Most of the vehicle owners had already been accounted for. Casey was more than happy to let uniform continue to work through the list.

But there was one name that drew her eye. A Toyota Corolla had been seen on camera driving away from the car park at 13.30 yesterday afternoon, just minutes after the figure she'd seen on the CCTV footage had come through the door of the ground floor exit.

If the driver — Karl Wallace, a check had revealed — and the suspect had crossed each other on the stairs, Wallace going up to the third floor to get his car, the other guy coming down, then Wallace might have seen the man's face just as clearly as she had. How did she feel about that though — Ella's rescuer perhaps being a killer too? She couldn't help hoping that he'd had nothing to do with this murder.

★ ★ ★

He'd stood at the window for a long time, peering through the curtains, waiting to see if she'd go away. He didn't like visitors. Not visitors who turned up in cars and parked outside his house. Man, woman, it was all the same these days. This one looked official. She looked Police. Don't ask him how he knew; he just did. He knew, too, that she wouldn't go away until he opened up. They never did go away. They hadn't last time when they'd come to tell him about Tony.

He'd had no choice but to let her in, in the end. Big smile, a flash of her I.D. They'd found him through his number plate, she said. She just needed to ask him a few questions. Then she mentioned the body. Had he heard? Jay Brennan, managed The Night Flower, that club down Devden way. No, he hadn't. He wasn't much of a clubber these days, he said. Kept his face deadpan. He was good at hiding things from people who wanted to get something out of you.

She had a nice face when she smiled. But he didn't trust her. Soon as her foot was over the threshold, she started eyeing up the framed photos on the mantelpiece.

'This your family, Mr Wallace?' she'd asked.

He'd wanted to tell her to get on with what she'd come for, nosy cow. Staring at that picture of Sarah and Tony as nippers, admiring his trophies in the glass-fronted cabinet he kept spit-spot, just like the house. Wanted to know if that was Henry Cooper with him in the photo. Seemed impressed when he admitted it was.

'What is it you want, Inspector?' he'd said in the end.

She'd been derailed by all his boxing memorabilia. People were. Not that he had that many visitors these days. She said there was a chance he'd crossed on the stairs with someone yesterday when he'd been going back for his car. He couldn't remember; he was minding his own business, he told her. Which was nothing but the truth.

When she showed him that computer printout, he spent a long time looking at it. Did he need to get his glasses, she asked him. He'd been sharp with her then. His eyes were as good now as they were twenty years ago. Thirty years ago, he said. Of course, she said, apologetic.

Wouldn't let it go when once again he said he'd seen nobody. Was he absolutely certain? He dug his heels in then. Why should he help the police? Even though he was doing himself no favours, being so awkward. What had they ever done for the likes of him, though? Always sniffing round this estate, they were, ready to pin some crime or other on the local lads. Easier to stop and search than to show them a bit of respect.

That had been *his* job. That's why he'd started up the boys' club all those years ago. Boxing. That gave you self-respect. You didn't need guns and knives when you knew how to duck and dive.

'I hope you find who you're looking for, Officer,' he told her, unable to suppress a small thrill at being able to disappoint her.

Trouble with the law was, they weren't as clever as they thought. They never asked the right questions, you see. She should have asked him if he knew Jay Brennan. Silly girl.

$\star \quad \star \quad \star$

When Casey rang home to make sure Dom had picked both kids up, she had a bit of explaining to do. Finlay and Ella, apparently, were playing a new game. 'Escape from the Burning Car' was its name. Which reminded him, had she gone off with his car this morning, because it didn't seem to be out front?

Dom had a tendency to overreact in situations where he thought Casey had been placed in danger. She knew it was only because he loved her, but even so. He was bound to blow a gasket if she told him the whole story, so she settled for the bare bones, before sneakily attempting to change the subject to her recent visit to Karl Wallace's house.

'Interesting old chap,' she said.

'Don't think you can sidetrack me so easily, Casey!'

'His living room was bursting with boxing memorabilia,' she persisted. 'There was even a framed photograph of him with Henry Cooper.'

'Finlay keeps throwing Patch behind the settee. Ella runs after Patch then Finlay runs after Ella. Says he's rescuing them.'

'Kids' games, Dom,' she said. 'Shows they've got healthy imaginations. Anyway, Karl Wallace. What do you know about him? He was blocking me, I'm convinced. I'd like to learn a bit more about him.'

During his time as staff reporter on the Brockhaven Gazette — a career Dom had swapped for the life of a freelance journalist, writer and sometime local radio broadcaster — there had been no subject he hadn't tackled. He'd always preferred the world of literature to that of sport, but even now, years after he'd quit writing the sports page, he still retained a huge amount of knowledge about the topic. Needless to say, he was in great demand at pub quizzes.

'Doesn't he run that boys' boxing club on the New Estate?'

The New Estate — so named because once upon a time, back in the fifties, it had been. Now, however, it was badly run down.

'There was something else too. Something about his son. Or grandson. Can't remember exactly, but you leave it with me.'

Casey metaphorically rubbed her hands in glee. If there was one thing that took Dom out of himself, it was a bit of research. He'd probably already put his worries about the welfare of his car and the kids behind him.

'You're a star,' she said, before hanging up. It was only then she remembered she hadn't asked him if there was any news about Michelle's baby.

★ ★ ★

What she'd really wanted when she'd driven over to The Night Flower was a good nosey round the flat where Brennan had lived. But the forensics team had laid claim to it first. Okay, she understood that, like her, they had a job to do, but a more territorial bunch she'd rarely encountered in all her years as a serving police officer.

They'd given her the usual line of being unwilling to risk contamination by allowing her inside Brennan's flat, alongside a promise that she would be the first to get a copy of their report once completed. Thereupon, she'd been summarily dismissed. No doubt they'd all had a giggle at her expense as soon as her back was turned.

Unwilling to return to the office, Casey stuck her head round the entrance to the bar itself. Initially, she'd been unable to pick out anything much in the gloom. Just the usual cluster of tables and the shadowy outlines of bottles and glasses. But then she became aware of the chink of glasses and the sound of running water. When Casey called out hello, a young woman emerged from behind the bar — tall and lean, a tea towel in one hand.

'You'll be with that lot, won't you?' she said, casting a wary glance at Casey before flicking a switch that illuminated the whole space.

Without giving Casey a chance to do anything other than flash her I.D., the girl launched into a stream of nervous chatter. She was all corners and angles, bristling with nerves, unable to keep her hands still, Casey observed. Was it shock or something else? Drugs, maybe? She'd seen that same wired intensity in cocaine users so many times in her line of work.

She didn't know why she'd come in, the girl said. There was nothing much to do, given what had happened. Oh, and she was Sarah, by the way. Acting manager. Well, she supposed she was now. That's what Head Office had said when she rang them to find out what she was supposed to do. She'd already told the other employees not to bother coming in. They wouldn't be opening until further notice.

'Out of respect,' she said.

There was a brief pause, in which Casey managed to ask Sarah how long she'd worked at The Night Flower (six years, came the answer), before she started up again.

'Want a drink?' Sarah was now back behind the bar. 'I'm having another, though I know I shouldn't. Fancy turning up dead in his car like that. Do you know who did it yet? He was a hard boss but a fair one, and as far as I know, he had no enemies.'

Casey shook her head, watching as Sarah reached for a glass and filled it with cola from the tap. No, nothing yet, but it was early days, she said, while wondering if perhaps it was simply a sugar rush she was suffering from. While Sarah's mouth was otherwise occupied, Casey slipped in another question. Could Sarah please give her the details of every employee, past and present; names, addresses and any other information she thought might be relevant.

'Already done,' she replied, putting down her glass and reaching for a bundle of forms in a buff folder behind her. 'Head Office said you'd want that. So I got it ready. There are photos too. But we don't keep records here longer than a year. You'll have to apply to the top if you want any older ones.'

'Well, this'll do for a start,' Casey said, surprised at the heaviness of the folder.

It seemed that nobody stayed long at The Night Flower.

★   ★   ★

Back at the station, Casey sat at her desk. An hour had passed. In that time, Casey had scrutinised over two dozen of the forms Sarah Parkinson had handed her. Some of the employees left of their own accord — at least half a dozen had left to go and work abroad, where presumably more money was to be made during the summer season than could ever be made in Devden — but quite a few had been sacked. It was this latter group that Casey singled out as being the most interesting. Revenge was a strong motive for murder. How had Sarah described Brennan? Hard, but fair. Ruthless, was the word Casey would have chosen. The guy seemed to be on some kind of power trip, if the number of minor misdemeanours that had resulted in people losing their jobs was anything to go by.

Someone had been sacked because he'd had his hand in the till and another for inappropriate behaviour towards a customer, which was fair enough. But what she picked out above all else was the number being dismissed for being five or ten minutes late for a shift; or for taking a few minutes too long on a break. In one case someone had lost their job because they'd been inappropriately dressed.

No warning, verbal or written had been given, as far as she could tell. One strike and you're out seemed to be Brennan's way. Couldn't that put someone's back up? Maybe not enough to kill him, but enough to goad a person into giving him a kicking. A kicking that maybe went a bit too far.

It was just as she was pondering the possibility of a disgruntled worker taking their revenge that she turned over the last form. The face in the photograph jumped out at her. Could it be? Her eyes scanned the name at the top of the form. Nicu

Corescu. Age 27. Employed as a doorman for six months, up until the 21st May. That was less than a week ago!

She groped in her bag for the printout of the composite she'd done earlier with Gail. There was definitely a likeness. As good a likeness as you'd ever get in a computerised picture based on a description of someone merely glimpsed in passing. The face was a little more jowly, perhaps, the hairline a touch higher, but maybe that was something to do with the angle from which this photo had been taken.

Casey rose from her desk, suddenly energised. She had an address for this guy. And with the reason for his dismissal staring up at her from the page, she had every reason to pay him a visit.

*　*　*

Pizza By The Shore was theoretically a misnomer. But it was near enough to the sea front, on a side street running back into the town, for Casey to let it go. The shop itself was closed for now, and access to the flat above it, where Nicu Corescu resided, according to the form with his name on, was round the back, through a small courtyard rammed with overflowing wheelie bins.

Casey wrinkled her nose and rang the bell. Her eye was drawn to the twitching of a curtain at an upstairs window. Then she heard footsteps clacking on uncarpeted stairs and the rattle of a bolt being drawn across the door lock.

She was immediately certain that the man who opened the door to her was not the man she remembered from this morning. He was taller, chunkier; older too. And the only thing he wore on his wrist was a watch. Casey couldn't help feeling relieved about that. All the same, he'd worked for Jay Brennan, and been sacked by him. Assaulting your boss enough to make his nose bleed was a pretty serious offence.

★   ★   ★

'Jay Brennan, *dead?*'
Casey had followed Nicu Corescu up

31

to his flat. The smell of stale pizza was everywhere and the tiny window in his poky, shabbily furnished flat, though open, did little to disperse the bad air.

He plonked himself down heavily on the edge of a sunken settee, over which a stripy throw had been thrown, presumably to hide the worn material beneath. Apart from a spotted mirror on the wall and a couple of non-descript pictures that presumably were part of the fixtures and fittings, there was very little else to look at here. A temporary home, was how Casey would have described it.

'You were sacked for taking a swing at your boss, weren't you?'

He looked up at her — she'd refused the seat he'd offered — and frowned, as his eyes flashed with sudden comprehension.

'Hey, wait a minute. What are you saying?'

'I'm not saying, I'm asking, Mr Corescu,' she corrected him.

The man's right leg began to quiver uncontrollably. He was clearly wound up.

And he was big and looked strong. Perhaps it had been a bad idea not to let them know back at the station where she was. Dom would kill her if anything happened to her.

'He owes me money,' he said. 'Now I'll never get it back.'

No expression of sorrow at the news. Well, that was honest of him, at least!

'Is that why you hit him?'

He nodded. 'He thinks he can pay me less than the English guys who work the door. I find out from one of other guys how much they get paid. So I go speak to him. Complain. He tell me if you don't like then you go back where you came from. So I hit him.'

'Right.'

'I didn't kill him. It was stupid thing to do. But I was angry. I was sorry straight away. I don't hit people.' He looked up at her with soft, scared, brown eyes.

'Where were you on Monday morning, sir?'

He let out a sigh of frustration. 'I was in bed. Because I have no work to go to,' he said. 'And I can't get work because he tell everyone what I did. He knows people.'

Interesting. What sort of people had Jay Brennan known, she wondered.

'I'm going back to my country,' he said. 'Nobody wants us here anyway.'

She felt for him. But she steeled herself. She was investigating a murder, after all.

'Don't try and do that just yet, would you, sir?' she said, turning to leave. 'I might have to pay you another visit.'

★ ★ ★

Dom and Finlay were alone at last, now Ella's granny had finally turned up to claim her. While Ella put on her shoes and retrieved her precious Patch, Dom ascertained that the new baby had still failed to put in an appearance. He closed the front door and leaned on it. The quiet was a blessed relief. How people coped with two kids he couldn't imagine.

Finlay, exhausted after all the revelry, had clambered onto the settee, and seemed content enough to simply sit and stare at the TV for half an hour before supper. Which gave Dom more than enough time to do his research.

It was the work of a moment to find the interview he was looking for. As soon as he'd put down the phone to Casey he'd remembered exactly what it was about Karl Wallace that was interesting. His son had died in tragic circumstances — a drunken brawl after a night out had led to him being fatally stabbed through an artery. There was some suspicion that he owed money, and that drugs were involved, but his father had sworn he was a loving, law-abiding son.

And here was the interview — a two-page spread in the Brockhaven Gazette, complete with photographs. Wallace inside the boys' boxing club he'd started, named after his son, to help young lads from the New Estate get a focus; Wallace in the ring facing an opponent in his glory days. And the biggest picture of all, a full page one of him at home in his living room, standing awkwardly with an arm around his seated teenage granddaughter, whom he'd brought up since her father's death. Her young mother, unable to cope on her own, had willingly given her up.

'Daddy! I'm hungry!'

'Right you are, buddy. Just give me a second to send this email to Mummy and I'll be all over it.'

'Tell her I love her too, Daddy, will you?'

Dom turned to grin at his son. 'Come and do it yourself,' he said. 'I'll show you which keys to press.'

Finlay's face lit up as he bounced off the sofa and ran towards him. Yep, one child was plenty for him. He couldn't imagine loving another one as much as he loved this little chap.

* * *

Stefan was tired. Bone tired. All he wanted to do was to crawl into the sleeping bag he called his bed. Nicu made him store it at the back of the cupboard so as not to alert the landlord that Stefan was living there with him. 'Before you know it, he'll be doubling my rent,' his brother had explained.

When Nicu still had his job at the bar, Stefan would take advantage of his absence and crawl into his brother's bed, after an uncomfortable and almost sleepless night on the floor, just to remind himself what sleeping in a real bed felt like. He was grateful to Nicu for putting him up while he looked for work and a place of his own. Or — what he really longed for — a bigger place the two of them could share. But he'd known from the start he was in the way. And now, after what he'd done, he was in the way more than ever.

He could sleep under the pier tonight, he supposed. But the nights were cold and there were guys down there he didn't like the look of. Perhaps if he went back and begged his brother to take him in again after their row, then Nicu would be shamed into remembering his promise to their mother, to look after his little brother when he came to England.

He'd been walking with his head down and his hood up to avoid attention, and hadn't noticed he'd reached the pizza place already. He could let himself in and try and talk to Nicu. Tell him he'd done what he'd done for *him*, because he'd been so angry about the way this guy he worked for had treated him. Make him understand.

Stefan walked round to the back entrance, but couldn't quite bring himself to step inside the courtyard. He looked up at the window, but there was no movement. Perhaps Nicu had gone out. Cautiously he stepped inside, taking hesitant steps towards the door. He felt for his key in his pocket.

Footsteps coming downstairs stopped him from using it. He held his breath, turning over in his mind the best phrase to have ready that would soften Nicu's heart towards him. Stefan could see the outline of a figure on the frosted glass. Any second now they would be face to face. He took a deep breath and closed his eyes, praying for the right words to come.

When he opened them, his fingers still clutching his key, he didn't understand why he was looking into the eyes of a woman and not Nicu. He recognised her right away, and was certain she recognised him too. For a moment the two of them stood stock still, locked on to each other's gaze. Then her eyes roamed over his face, before travelling to his arm, still outstretched, his sleeve riding up exposing his lucky bracelet — one of the girls in the village had given it to him when she'd learned he was travelling to the UK to join his brother and find work.

Why was she here? How had she found him? Did she want to give him a reward? But he couldn't take a reward; he couldn't have his face in the papers. He wasn't meant to be here in this country; they'd send him back, and then his brother would get into trouble too, for housing him. As if he needed any more reasons for Nicu to be angry with him!

His heart pounding fiercely, he turned on his heels and fled. He heard her swearing softly as he cleared the yard, turned the corner and headed towards the sea front. Seconds later he heard her footsteps behind him.

Immediately, he knew it had been a

stupid, stupid idea to take this direction. He couldn't run on the sand, not in these cheap trainers. He'd just have to pray she was a poor runner. Women her age were, it was a fact. But with every step he took he felt her getting closer. And now she was shouting something. Stop! Police!

Stefan panicked but kept on running. But then the worst thing happened. His right shoelace, which he was always having to bend down and re-tie, had come undone again. Too late to do anything about it, he tripped over it, falling heavily on the pavement. He lay there, afraid to look up. His knee hurt and a staggering pain ripped through his side.

'Stay where you are, young man,' he heard the woman say. 'My name's Detective Inspector Casey Clunes. And you're nicked.'

$\star$ $\star$ $\star$

'I just can't believe that a guy who would pull a kid out of a burning car one minute would murder someone the next.'

40

Casey was on her third coffee of the morning. If there'd been a way of getting it intravenously, then she'd have tried it. She and Gail had had ten minutes with Stefan Corescu, during which time all he'd said was, 'I want my brother.' The Romanian translator was earning easy money this morning.

Gail, much more sensibly, was drinking Red Bush. But then, Gail hadn't been up late into the night toasting the arrival of a new baby boy with a neighbour who was on such a high that the only thing that would bring him back down was a party.

A sensible friend would have advised a hot bath, a glass of warm milk and sleep. Dom cracked open a bottle of wine. And another. When the whiskey came out, Casey, remembering that she had a job to do, crawled off to bed, leaving the boys to it.

'Strictly speaking, if he *is* guilty, he committed the murder first. It was a day later he rescued Ella. Maybe he was atoning for his sins.'

Casey considered this option. It was a reasonable one. Even the worst criminals and tyrants had their redeeming features. Hitler loved animals; the Kray twins adored their mother. With a sigh, she picked up a random photo of the car in which Jay Brennan's body had been discovered — one of many taken from different angles. It was an Audi RS6, all bells and whistles and dark glass.

'This scratch goes all the way round the body of the car,' she said. 'Whoever killed him was emphasising just how much they didn't like the guy, I'd say.'

Gail agreed. 'I just wish we had more to go on,' she said. 'The lighting is so bad in that place, and their CCTV system is about ten years out of date. I could take clearer pictures with my old Brownie.'

Casey nodded in agreement. 'Car's crawling with DNA too. It'll take months to identify which bit belongs to who.'

It was clear that they were just going to have to rely on old-fashioned policing. Casey's phone bleeped. It was front office. An extremely agitated Nicu Corescu had been brought in. He could see his brother for five minutes, Casey agreed. But only with the interpreter present. And he wasn't to think for a second that the buck had stopped with Stefan. She still had her beady eye on him.

'You ready for this, then, Gail?' Casey drained the last of her coffee and, crushing the container, took aim at the bin in the corner.

It missed.

'Don't think I don't know what you're doing,' Gail said, rising from her seat. 'If it goes in they're guilty. If it misses they're innocent.'

Casey had been rumbled. It was a silly superstition, she knew. But so far in her career she'd only been wrong twice. Of course, they did say that everything came in threes.

★ ★ ★

'Grandad?' Sarah's voice was shaky, though she was trying hard to steady it. If Grandad knew she'd taken something, he'd go ballistic. You couldn't even have a discussion with him about drugs. As far as he was concerned, drugs killed people. He wouldn't listen to any arguments about how, if you legalised them, people would know what they were getting, and there'd be no need for cartels and gangs.

It was drugs that had done for Dad. Mum had been wasted on them too, which is why she'd been so keen to give her away after Dad's death. God only knew where she was now. Probably in the gutter. It was no loss — Grandad had turned out to be a better parent than either of hers had ever been. Fact.

'Sarah. Wassup?'

She smiled at his attempts to be cool. Nobody had said Wassup since the nineties.

'I just needed to hear your voice,' she said. 'I'm not feeling too good, to be honest.'

There was a pause. Did she imagine it, or could she really discern everything he was thinking and feeling on the other side of the line? That he loved her, worried for her, was there for her. She didn't need words. Which was just as well, as Grandad was no talker.

'Just do your job, Sarah. Stay cool.

That's all you need to do.'

She nodded. She understood that that was all the comfort she was going to get. It was clear Grandad was at the club. He was devoted to his lads, as he called them. She could make out the grunts and thumps in the background, boxers knocking seven bells out of each other.

A gentleman's sport, Grandad always called it. His lads always wore gum shields and head protection. So different from what happened on the estate. You stepped out of line once, you got a pasting. More and you got a knife, like Dad had. Grandad said in boxing there was no hitting below the belt. Someone should have told Jay Brennan that. He might still be alive if they had.

* * *

Casey hated speaking through interpreters. It took too long, for a start, and the time delay made it impossible to read not only faces but the silences between the exchanges. She was never one hundred per cent certain, either, exactly how accurate the interpreter was. Not everybody was as predisposed towards the police as your average, middle-class white person, she was well aware of that. What if the guy repeating Stefan's assertion that he'd never heard of Jay Brennan, and never been near his car, was on his side and deliberately changing his words to paste over any glaring slip-ups?

Gail reached for the still that showed Stefan Corescu pushing through the ground floor door of the car park — about the only halfway decent bit of pictorial evidence they'd been able to come up with so far.

'Is this you?' she said.

Stefan didn't need anyone to translate that particular question — not with the evidence staring him in the face. He looked as guilty as hell.

'Okay,' he said. 'Let me explain.'

At last, thought Casey.

'Take your time,' she said.

Stefan composed himself. 'My brother. I love him,' he began, in English. 'He help me when I come here. Gave me place to

46

sleep. Money. Food. He had good job . . . '

But when Nicu walked out of his job after his boss had insulted him by telling him he should go back to his own country if he wasn't happy with the money he was getting, Stefan had grown anxious and afraid. He couldn't get a job himself because his English was too poor; he'd run out of his savings and he wasn't eligible for benefits.

'I visited Nicu's bar, don't ask me why,' he said, through the interpreter. 'I tried to talk to this man, this boss. I begged him to take Nicu back. This time it was my face he laughed at, not Nicu's. I wanted to kill him. How dare he be so contemptuous?'

Hurt pride and fury were written all over his face.

'There he was with his big car and his flashy watch and there we were with nothing,' he said. 'When he kicked me out I was mad at him. I needed to do something to get rid of my anger and to show him he couldn't walk all over my family just like that.'

'So, what did you do?'

His eyes grazed the floor. When he mumbled something the interpreter had to ask him to repeat it.

'He says he keyed the bodywork on the car belonging to Jay Brennan, before running off,' the man said.

That was one thing cleared up, then.

'So tell me what you were doing in the car park, Mr Corescu, the day Jay Brennan's body was found,' she said. 'Did you see Mr Brennan's car parked on the top floor?'

'Yes,' he said. 'I saw it.'

'Did you approach it?'

He shook his head. No, he didn't want anything more to do with that man. He'd made his point, he said.

'It was a bit of a coincidence though, wasn't it? You both being in the same place at the same time. Why were you there?'

Stefan shifted in his seat and looked down at his interlaced fingers for a long time. Again, he spoke so quietly he was asked to say it twice. The interpreter looked shocked at what he'd heard.

'What is it?' Casey glanced from one to the other of the two men. 'What did he say?'

'He said he went to the car park, all the way up to the top floor, because he'd decided to jump.'

* * *

Casey needed a break after her interview with Stefan, some space and time to herself to try to sift out the truth of everything he'd told her. Her instinct was to believe him — and not just because she'd missed the wastepaper basket.

She visualised him climbing all the way up to the top floor, walking up to the edge, looking down and thinking what a mess his life was. No money, no job and no prospect of either. Knowing that if he stayed in the UK, sooner or later he'd end up on the street, and that if he returned to his country people would know he'd been unable to make a go of it.

It made sense, too, how badly affected he'd been by Nicu accusing Stefan of humiliating him. Casey had seen the two

49

of them together only briefly, but it was plain to see how much Stefan craved his older brother's approval. After their last argument, Stefan had run out of the flat in despair, Nicu's furious words still ringing in his ears, he'd told them.

That's when he'd ended up where he had. And it was just as he was about to jump that he noticed Jay Brennan's car, parked a few metres away from where he stood. In that moment, he'd realised something. Jay Brennan was not going to win again. He was going to continue to live.

He knew it even more the next morning, when, after a sleepless night spent on the beach, he'd seen the little girl in trouble in the car. Life was just too precious to throw away, he said. If Casey had needed any more convincing, then his humble words had done the trick. But there was still a killer out there somewhere and she needed a lead.

Casey had arrived late at work this morning, after the revelry of the previous night. Too late to check her email before Gail turned up with her second coffee of the day, having gulped down the first while simultaneously running around the house putting it to rights and yelling at Dom that he only had himself to blame for his present fragile state. Clicking on it now, she was surprised to see a message, with an attachment, from Dom, sent late the previous afternoon. What was he doing sending her mail? She clicked on it. The message was short. 'Is this any use to you?'

Of course — she'd asked him to try and find out something about Karl Wallace. She hadn't liked the man's evasiveness but she had nothing on him, other than that his car had been seen leaving the car park just minutes after Stefan Corescu. But if Stefan was off the hook then she might just as well discount Wallace too and kill two birds with one stone.

She almost missed the P.S. in her keenness to download the attachment. Almost, but not quite. 'P.S. Mummy I love you and I am being a good boy. Come home soon, Finlay xxx'

With a broad smile on her face, and

touched by Finlay's words, Casey downloaded the attachment and opened it. The smile froze on her face as soon as she saw the picture of Karl Wallace sitting in his living room, his granddaughter perched on the arm of his chair.

She knew that girl. She'd interviewed her the day before. Sarah Parkinson was the name she'd given, not Wallace. Her mother's name, perhaps?

The coincidence was just too overwhelming. Jay Brennan, found dead in his car; Karl Wallace, seen driving his car away from there; finally, his granddaughter, who worked in the very same bar Brennan ran.

At that moment, Gail popped her head round the door. 'You need to hear this, Casey,' she said. 'There's a Sarah Parkinson at the front desk. She says she killed Jay Brennan.'

*   *   *

Wednesday was Sarah's day for coming over to do his washing and a bit of dusting. He was worried about her after her phone call. He should have listened to his instincts and gone to see her. But he was in the middle of a training session. He couldn't just leave, he had a reputation for being reliable.

That's why she'd rung him from the car park on Monday afternoon. 'Grandad, you've got to come. Something's happened. Something bad.' As luck would have it, he was already on the way up the stairs to pick up his car after he'd done his bit of food shopping. Stay calm, he said. Get back in the car, shut the door and wait for me.

Lucky, too, that there was no one about, bar that one lad he'd crossed on the stairs with. He'd got in his car, driven it up the ramp to the top floor and there he found her, sobbing in the passenger seat, clutching a ruddy great bottle of champagne in her hands and staring into space. Him, next to her, slumped over the wheel. Dead as a doornail.

It was an accident, she'd told him. She'd lost her rag with Brennan because he'd started bragging about the profits he made from kids wanting to buy drugs at the club. She hadn't meant to thump him. But he'd lied to her, all those promises he'd clean the place up.

The bottle of champagne was the first thing she'd picked up; it was just lying there in the back seat and he'd been grinning at her, like he couldn't care less about the struggles people had with drugs, just as long as he could make a profit from it.

She knew about those struggles, did Sarah, with a mum on the scrap heap and her father killed because he hadn't the money to pay back his drug debts. And don't think Karl didn't know she had her own struggles. He'd seen the signs, hoped he'd got it wrong. Known he was kidding himself.

The house was quiet as he let himself in. Usually, when Sarah was here, she played loud music and there was the sound of water running or the vacuum cleaner doing its work, and the smell of polish in the air. But not this morning. The curtains were still closed and the remains of his breakfast lay where he'd left them.

He strode over to the phone, ill at ease.

There was a message for him, just as he'd suspected there would be. Received at 08.33, according to the soulless voice that repeated it. It was Sarah.

'Grandad, I'm going to the police. I thought I could carry on as usual. But I can't. I'm sorry.'

He replaced the receiver with a shaky hand, his mouth dry with foreboding. He needed to sit down to stop the room spinning round him. Was this what getting old felt like? he wondered. This sudden grip of ice-cold fear that the best of life was behind you? She couldn't go down for this. She was all he had left.

★ ★ ★

The pull of family was strong. Even as Sarah was being led away after being cautioned, Karl Wallace came crashing through the main entrance insisting he'd been the one to slam the champagne bottle into the back of Jay Brennan's head.

It was a good try, but the only thing that had changed was that he'd been

55

charged with conspiracy to pervert the course of justice. Sarah Parkinson was lucky to have someone in her life prepared to do time on her behalf. That was family loyalty in the extreme.

The thought of family loyalty persuaded Casey to make a phone call and one final visit before she headed home for the evening. Once again she retraced her footsteps to *Pizza By The Shore*, dodging the overflowing bins in the little courtyard, averting her eyes at the sight of a big ugly rat scurrying off into the undergrowth.

The two brothers had left separately after they'd been interviewed, Nicu hurrying away, head down without a glance at his brother, who'd watch him leave with sadness in his eyes.

'You here to arrest me again?' Nicu said, when he answered the door.

So, somewhere deep inside this moody man who seemed so full of resentment, there lurked a sense of humour.

'I need to tell you something about your brother,' she said. 'And I'd like to help him, if only I knew where I could find him.'

He shrugged. 'Don't ask me. That boy is a pain. Sticking his nose in where he has no business. Always the same, act first, think second.'

'It's because he acted before he thought that a little girl is alive today.'

He stared at her, a puzzled frown on his face.

'Your brother is a hero, Mr Corescu,' she said. 'If you let me in, then I'll tell you all about it.'

★   ★   ★

'You really are an old softy, you know.'

Casey and Dom were drinking wine. The lights were dim, the curtains closed, Finlay was tucked up in bed and all was right with the world.

'They're the only family each other has.' Casey tucked her legs under her on the settee. 'And I know someone who's looking for a couple of seasonal workers on his farm. They won't be able to stay in the country once the season's over, but if they work hard then future employment will be guaranteed. They'll have a job and

57

a place to live over here for three months every year.'

Dom smiled and closed his eyes.

'So now you've sorted that family out, what are we going to do about this one?'

Next door's baby was home at last and he'd taken Finlay to see it. The little boy hadn't been very impressed, apparently.

'He says he's changed his mind about having a baby sister or brother,' Dom said. 'He'd rather have a dog.'

'So the pressure's off, then,' Casey said.

She didn't quite know how she felt about that. A new baby would be hard work, of course. But still . . .

'Except,' Dom said, 'when I saw that little baby lying there with his starfish hands and his little perfect mouth, I suddenly remembered what it is about babies that makes them so special.'

'So, what are you saying?' She suddenly felt all warm and fuzzy.

'I'm not sure.' Dom reached for the bottle. 'Maybe that I'm open to discussion.'

'Well, that's a start,' she said, holding out her glass.

Casey in the Saddle

'Why can't we have a dog?'

Finlay sat across the table from Casey, his huge brown eyes, the spit of Dom's, challenging her to come up with a convincing reason. She could tell he was serious about this. His current favourite supper — macaroni cheese — remained untouched in front of him. Usually he wolfed it down in seconds.

'It wouldn't be fair,' Casey said. 'You're out at school all day. Mummy's out at work. Who'd look after him?'

'There's Dad,' Finlay said. 'He could keep him company and I'd take him for walks when I got back from school and in the holidays.'

'Dad's not here every day,' Casey replied. 'You know he sometimes has to go away for this and that. And if you took the dog out for a walk, you wouldn't be able to go far on your own without an adult.'

'Well, you could come with me. When you got back from work.'

'Dogs need routine, Finlay. They need to be fed and walked at regular times. We're not really that great on routine in this family, what with my job and everything, are we?'

Finlay sighed. 'It's not fair,' he said.

'Maybe not. But neither would it be fair to make a dog live somewhere where the family couldn't look after him as well as he deserved.'

Finlay was a reasonable child compared to many she'd encountered. He could see this, surely?

'Everybody has a dog,' he said, lifting his fork dejectedly.

Bang went that theory, then.

'Go on then,' she challenged. 'Tell me who you know who has a dog.'

No more than three families at the most among his pool of friends, she was certain.

'I'm eating,' he said. 'You said it was bad manners to talk with your mouth full.'

Touché, thought Casey. Finlay was

eight. Heaven help them all when he became a teenager. She glanced at the kitchen clock. Was it too early to open that bottle of wine?

* * *

The next day, at lunchtime in the station canteen, Casey found herself discussing the previous evening's conversation with her friend and colleague, Gail Carter.

'What does Dom think?' Gail asked, peering at the contents of her baguette with forensic scrutiny.

Since last month, when someone had discovered a small, crawling thing in their salad, examining any food bought in the canteen had become an epidemic. If they were as vigilant searching for criminals as they were looking for imaginary creepy crawlies in everything they ate, crime would soon become a thing of the past in these parts, so the Super joked.

'Dom thinks we should get him a hamster or a guinea pig,' Casey said.

'Not a dog?'

Casey shook her head.

'Because?'

'Well, I guess he agrees with me. For once.'

Gail grinned. 'So why don't you compromise with a hamster?' she said, her eyes not leaving her baguette.

Casey didn't want to say. She had a reputation to maintain as a tough cookie who could strike fear into the hearts of even the most hardened offender once she got them inside an interview room.

'Gail, I'm sure that baguette is perfectly okay for you to eat,' she said.

Gail glanced up and fixed Casey with a suspicious glare.

'Come on. Answer my question.'

'What question?'

'Hamsters. Guinea pigs. You're scared of them aren't you?'

'No!' Casey's protest came out as an unconvincing squeak.

'Ha! I don't believe you,' Gail replied.

Admitting defeat, Casey threw up her hands in surrender. Gail had missed her vocation. She should have been a prosecution barrister.

'Okay, okay! I hate them. Skittering little long-tailed critters with twitchy noses and scratchy claws. The thought of picking one up!' She shuddered dramatically.

'I knew it!' Gail chuckled delightedly.

'Everybody's scared of something,' Casey said. 'It's only natural.'

'True. And they wouldn't be my pets of choice either, to be honest. Oh, and if you're worried I'll blackmail you to keep your secret away from the rest of the nick, there's no need.'

'Well, that's a relief.' Casey raised her glass to her lips. 'I'm paying a fortune already in hush money.'

They both chuckled.

'But, seriously, have you thought about a horse?'

Casey, in the process of swallowing a mouthful of water, almost choked at the suggestion.

'I'm not suggesting you buy one, idiot!' Gail said. 'But I take Molly riding sometimes. She gets to learn about respecting other creatures while learning a skill at the same time.'

Casey felt herself grow interested.

'And it keeps all the 'Mummy, can I have dog/cat/chicken/whatever, conversations at bay,' Gail went on. 'Because no animal can compete with a horse.'

There was some truth in this, she had to agree.

'Where do you go?' Casey wanted to know.

'Sycamore Stables and Riding School,' Gail replied. 'Out by Oakham Manor.'

'I know it.'

'Look. It's half term next week. You said you had a couple of days off. Well, so have I. I've already booked a half hour session at the stables for Molly on Monday. Why don't you do the same for Finlay? See if you can't cure him of his dog craving? We'll go together.'

'I'll think about it,' Casey said. 'Oh! What's that? Little black thing. It's just gone in your mouth!'

Gail, horrified snatched up a paper napkin.

'Only joking,' Casey said, before her friend could spit out her lunch. 'It was a speck of black pepper, that's all.'

66

Gail's suggestion had already started working, it seemed, before Finlay's little toes had even made it anywhere near a stirrup. From the very first moment Casey mentioned riding lessons, he hadn't brought up dogs once. In fact, he'd spent most of the previous weekend galloping round the garden, alternating between making clip-clopping sounds and whinnying noises of such convincing credibility that Casey had stuck her head out of the window at least twice to check there wasn't a pony in her back garden.

It was Gail's suggestion that the four of them went on their half term jaunt in her car. Casey was glad to see that Molly — whose spirits were as high as Finlay's this morning — was dressed as he was, in trainers, jeans and T-shirt, her jacket slung over her lap.

'I was afraid she'd be all togged up in jodhpurs and hacking jacket,' Casey said, clambering into the front passenger seat, once she'd made sure Finlay was secure in the back.

'God, no,' Gail said. 'Sycamore Stables is nothing like that. In fact it's a bit of a dump. I think the owner had aspirations for it at one time. But the money must have run out or something.'

'So no yummy mummies and Jemimas then?'

'Oh, sure. You get the odd few,' Gail said. 'I think their kids have proper lessons, though. Learn how to jump and take part in gymkhanas and all that.'

'So why doesn't Molly do that?'

They were on the road to Devden now. It was only ten o'clock but already the sun was bursting through the clouds and the day promised to be fine and warm.

'Molly hasn't got a competitive bone in her body,' Gail said. 'Add to that the fact that her mother was forced not only to do ballet but music lessons, for far too many years, very much against her will, and there you have your reason.'

Casey took a similar view herself. Finlay's hobbies tended to come and go, but so far nothing had stuck apart from his love of eating and making a mess in his room.

'If she wants to take it more seriously down the line then she can. Until then, it's just a bit of fun,' Gail added. 'Oh, look! Here we are.'

A home-made sign pointed down a narrow turning to the stables. They came off the main road, bumping and bouncing their way along the uneven, stony path.

'Now I see why you suggested your car and not mine,' Casey said, clutching onto the dashboard of Gail's SUV. 'Perhaps a couple of hard hats might not have come amiss after all.'

The kids, who thought the ride was great fun, squealed loudly in the back. By the time they pulled up on a piece of rough ground, Casey's ears were ringing with their racket. A couple of other vehicles were already on the makeshift car park, but there was no sign of anyone else apart from them. The whole place had rather a neglected air, Casey thought.

As they scrambled down from the car they were met by the pungent, yet not — at least to Casey's nose — unpleasant smell of horse manure. Predictably, this set the children off shrieking once more.

'Oh, poo!' Molly squealed, clutching her nose and staggering about like she'd been pelted with the stuff.

'Smelly poo! Smelly poo!' Finlay joined in, waving his arms around madly.

The two of them were as high as kites and they hadn't even got on a horse yet. A glance at Gail, who rolled her eyes in despair that two such sensible women could produce such badly behaved offspring, suggested she felt just the same — that there was a fairly good chance this morning's outing would end in tears.

'Come on,' Casey said, as they trudged up the small incline towards the main house in search of anyone who might be in charge. 'And calm down you two, or you'll frighten the horses.'

A young woman, her jeans tucked into her wellies and her hair tied back, sat perched on a stool in the stable yard, running a brush over a handsome bay. The horse glared at them with huge eyes before shaking its magnificent head and snorting disdainfully. 'If you think I'd let one of those unruly children onto my back, you've got another think coming,' he seemed to say.

The girl looked up, put down her brush and removed her earphones.

'Good girl, Stardust,' she said, giving the horse a friendly pat. 'You here for a session? Have you booked?'

Casey gave their names.

'You need to come up to the house first so I can book you in,' the girl said. 'I don't know where everybody else is. Sadie should be around to take one of the children, and I'm down to do the other. I'm Kelly, by the way.'

Although she spoke politely enough, Casey couldn't help picking up a touch of resentment in the girl's manner. Unsurprising, since she appeared to have been left in sole charge.

Between them, Casey and Gail agreed that Casey would make the short walk to the house to do the paperwork. Meanwhile, Gail would wait with the children and keep them entertained.

'Good luck with that one,' Casey muttered, hurrying to catch up with Kelly, who was striding ahead.

'Mrs Cassidy must be out somewhere,'

she said, wiping her feet before stepping inside the tiny room that looked like it doubled as a kitchen as well as an office. 'She's the boss,' Kelly added, noticing Casey's blank face. 'Right, then . . . if you're booked in then your details should be on the computer.'

'Right,' Casey said.

'I'll just see if either of them are around upstairs first,' the girl said, disappearing up some stairs.

Casey, left behind, glanced around. A smell of damp and an air of general despondency emanated from the room. A vase of dead flowers and some unwashed mugs in the sink added to the atmosphere of neglect.

If this didn't get sorted out soon then Casey was going to have to suggest something else to the children. Was there a farm round here where they could go and stroke a few lambs or watch some cows being milked, she wondered. One thing was certain, Molly and Finlay would not be content to just get back in the car, turn round and drive home. The floor above her head creaked as Kelly went from room to room, calling out for Mrs Cassidy and Sadie — alas, to no avail.

Outside, the sound of the children playing grew louder and more manic. She thought she heard Gail calling them to stay put and not to stray. But if they heard her they'd obviously decided to take no notice because she called out again, louder this time, and more exasperated.

What she heard next chilled her to the bone — the sound of hooves pounding on the ground, children screaming, Gail yelling. Instinct kicked in, propelling her towards the door, her blood thumping in her ears.

She saw the horse. She saw her son standing directly in its path as it hurtled towards him. Her brain told her it was impossible. She couldn't reach him in time. But still, she ran. All she knew was that she had to get to him before the horse did.

What happened next was over in an instant. She saw Gail throw herself at Finlay, grab him in both arms and pin his small body to her own, her momentum carrying them both out of harm's way. A split second later, and the horse would have trampled them to the ground.

'Finlay! Finlay!'

Casey was still running, her breath coming in painful bursts. She had a stitch in her side and sweat was pouring from her. She was vaguely aware of someone else running too. It was Kelly. One final spurt and he was in reach of her arms.

'It's all right. It's all right,' Gail said, pale and shaking. 'He's safe.'

Casey made a lunge for him, grabbing hold of him and holding him tight. Over and over she murmured that he was safe, that there was no need for him to be frightened, that she had him and was never going to let him go.

Gail, meanwhile, had sunk to her knees on the ground beside them, her face ashen. Casey was vaguely aware that Kelly had run past them without pausing, and was still going. But right now that wasn't her concern.

'Molly!' Gail suddenly began to struggle

to her feet, her voice high-pitched and full of panic. 'Where's Molly? Have you seen her?'

Casey, continuing to hold onto a still-stunned Finlay, turned her head this way and that. There was no sign of Molly anywhere. Had the horse . . . ? She didn't dare even ask the question, let alone answer it. How unforgivable of her. She'd been so concerned about the safety of her own child that she'd forgotten all about Gail's.

'I . . . No. I'll go and look for her.'

She owed her best friend this at least. Gail had saved Finlay's life.

'No,' Gail replied. 'I'll go.'

But as soon as she took a step forward her body began to fold. Casey let go of Finlay, telling him not to move, and dashed to her friend's aid, catching her before she reached the ground.

'I've got you, Gail,' she said.

'Did you see the little girl?' she called out to Kelly, who was standing at a distance with the horse, watching them. It was clear where her priorities lay. Not with the humans, who, apart from suffering shock, were all in one piece, but with the animal that'd bolted off like that.

The horse was docile now, its head lowered obediently, responding to Kelly's soothing murmuring. It wasn't the horse they'd seen when they first arrived but another; heavier, stockier, grey. Where it had appeared from, Casey had no idea.

'No, I'm sorry,' the girl replied. 'I'm going to take him to his stable. Then I'll help look for her. I'll be as quick as I can.'

'I'm certain Molly's safe,' Casey said, though she had no way of knowing this for sure, and probably shouldn't have said it. But she had to keep Gail calm somehow.

'How do you know?' Gail got to her feet unsteadily. 'That horse came out of nowhere. The kids — they both went running off. They wouldn't listen to me. What if it knocked her down before it headed this way?'

Finlay's eyes suddenly welled up with tears. 'I'm sorry,' he said.

Immediately, Gail had Finlay in an embrace. 'No,' she said. 'Don't be sorry.

76

It's not your fault. You didn't make Molly run off.'

'Let me go and look for her. Please,' Casey said. 'Stay here. Both of you.'

But there was no need for Casey to go anywhere. Because here was Molly herself, wandering nonchalantly towards them from the direction of the stables. Gail sprinted towards her, lifting the bemused Molly right off her feet and holding her so tightly, she begged to be put down.

'Mummy, stop it. You're being silly,' Molly cried.

'I know, I know,' Gail said. 'But I can't help it.'

Finally she let Molly go.

'Where did you get to?' Casey wanted to know. 'Did you see the horse running?'

Molly nodded.

'And I heard it roaring,' she said. 'I was hiding from it.'

'Good girl.' Casey and Gail spoke at the same time.

'Horses don't roar,' Finlay said, disdainfully. 'Lions and tigers roar. Horses whinny.'

'That's enough, Finlay,' Casey said, sharply. 'Nobody likes a clever clogs.'

But Molly was a sweet-natured girl. She never minded being corrected.

'Whinny, then,' she said.

Turning to Gail, Casey said, 'Well, I don't know about you, but I think I'm done with horses for today.'

'I don't think I actually like horses very much,' Finlay piped up. 'I think I'd actually rather have a dog.'

Casey and Gail exchanged rueful glances.

'You lot stay here while I catch Kelly up and tell her we've decided to give it a miss,' Casey said. 'Better still, go and sit in the car. All of you. Just in case there are any more stray horses on the rampage.'

She did her best to inject her words with a light tone. They'd all had a shock — Finlay and Gail had undergone a life-threatening incident. With a bit of luck and a touch of humour, Finlay might never realize just how close he'd come to being trampled to death.

Feeling weary to her bones, Casey

made her way over to the stable block. As she neared it, she heard music playing — classical stuff, something she recognized but couldn't put a name to. Perhaps this was Kelly's way of helping the horse remain calm after it had bolted.

What made a horse bolt, she wondered? Something must have spooked it to make it go off like that.

'Kelly?'

Kelly, her back towards Casey, was standing in the middle of the yard, still holding onto the reins of the grey pony. It was as if she'd been struck dumb by something, because she didn't respond when Casey called her name. She tried again. This time Kelly did turn round.

'Look,' she said.

At first, Casey couldn't work out what she was pointing at. Was it the stable door that — from the look of it — had been totally destroyed, bits of it spread out all over the ground? She moved nearer and took a peek into the stable.

It smelled warm and of animal. But it was a complete disaster zone, with tools and straw scattered everywhere. And then she saw it. A boot. With a foot inside it. A leg attached to the foot. And then another leg. And a hand. And something that looked suspiciously like blood.

'I think it must be Sadie,' Kelly whispered, the colour draining from her face.

★ ★ ★

You had to hand it to Dom. He was your man in a crisis. He didn't bat an eyelid when Casey got on the phone to ask him to drop everything and come and get the children because there'd been a terrible accident, and Gail and she were needed at the stables to deal with the fall-out.

He was there within half an hour, arriving moments before the ambulance and — in another vehicle — a doctor. When one of the children wanted to know if the ambulance was for the horse that had gone a bit crazy, Dom said yes without blinking.

He led them both off, promising a pub lunch followed by a few hours on the beach collecting shells. Watching the children skipping off happily while competing for Dom's attention with their happy chatter, Casey convinced herself that Finlay hadn't suffered any ill effects from his recent near-death experience. If there was any fear bubbling beneath his cheerful surface, the time to expect it would be sometime between bedtime and the middle of the night. She was ready for it.

Gail had led Kelly away from the scene and up to the main house, allowing the groom to get a close enough look at the body to be able to identify it as that of her co-worker, but making sure she didn't get close enough to see the damage Sadie's small frame had sustained. No doubt she was, at this very moment, persuading Kelly to drink a cup of over-sweet tea for the shock.

So, with Gail otherwise occupied and Dom and the kids gone, it fell to Casey to accompany the GP back to the stables to complete the unenviable task of writing the death certificate. The ambulance crew followed close behind. It would be their job to transport the body to the morgue for the post-mortem.

Dr Grant was a benign-looking man, with a face as crumpled as his suit. As they picked their way through the bits of the broken stable door to the body, Casey filled him in on the little she knew so far about the victim.

'Sadie Warren,' she said. 'Kelly — the girl's co-worker — knew it was her immediately. She'd missed her earlier in the day. Thought the girl was skiving, but was too busy to leave the new stable block where she was working to trek all the way over here to look for her.'

Sadie's body lay uncovered now, one boot on, the other somewhere out of sight. She was dressed in a pair of dirty jeans and a T-shirt splattered in a mixture of dirt and blood, her arms scarred and bruised. They both agreed it looked like the horse had got spooked and lashed out with his hooves, and that Sadie had, unfortunately, happened to be in the way.

'There's a dent here, just above her left temple,' he said, kneeling down to examine her more closely. 'I couldn't say for sure, but in all probability her death will have been caused by inter-cranial bleeding.'

There would have to be an autopsy, of course, and the coroner's office would need the name of her next of kin, he said. Then he turned his attention to the horse. Where was it? And how was it? Had they called the vet? When Casey admitted it hadn't occurred to her, he said she should — a vet might be able to explain why the horse had behaved the way he had that morning.

Casey added 'find out the name of the vet from Kelly' to her mental list of things to do. Easing himself slowly up off the ground, Dr Grant reached for his bag, drew out a pad and proceeded to scribble in it, before signalling for the ambulance men to step forward to remove the body.

With one last, lingering look at the corpse as the two men lifted it respect-fully onto the stretcher before covering it up, Casey, who was not a particularly religious person, offered up a silent prayer that the girl's demise had been instant, and that she hadn't been frightened when she drew her last breath.

At Casey's behest, a couple of uniformed officers had been summoned and
were now stationed at the entrance to the
Stables, their brief being to head off all
those who turned up expecting a riding
lesson. As far as the public was
concerned, today the school was closed.

Casey, safe in the knowledge she wasn't
the only one holding the fort, grabbed the
opportunity to slip over to the house to
find out from a still-shaken Kelly the
name of the vet's practice they used.

She needed Sadie's parents' address
too, since the sooner they were informed
the better.

But that was information known only
to Emma Cassidy, who still hadn't shown
her face.

Casey was coming out of the house
when she spotted a woman in full jogging
gear running in her direction. She looked
to be in some pain, like she'd run her
heart out and was now on the point of
collapse. Casey guessed who this was
immediately. Uniform wouldn't have let
just anyone in.

The woman came to a halt in front of

her, gripped her knees and leaned forward, dropping her head as she struggled to calm her rasping breath.

'Mrs Cassidy?' Casey said, addressing the woman's back.

Emma Cassidy, finally in control of her breathing, lifted her head. 'Sorry,' she gasped. 'Training. Half marathon. Next week. I just heard what happened. Where's Chanter?'

'Chanter?'

'The horse. They said he bolted.'

Most people would have asked about the dead person first, Casey mused. People who put the welfare of animals before that of human beings were an alien bunch in her view, but she was well aware that they existed. And here — so it seemed — was a prime example.

'He's fine. Unlike Sadie,' she said, pointedly.

'Oh God. I'm sorry.' The woman straightened up at last. 'It's just — well, I can't get my head round it. Can I see her?'

Casey explained that the body had just been removed, and that a post-mortem would be taking place.

'Post-mortem? They said it was an accident.'

She began to carry out a series of stretches, of the kind inflicted on Casey at the end of her weekly aerobics class. While Emma Cassidy completed her quad stretches, Casey — thinking how utterly bizarre it was to be talking about such a sombre subject with a woman who was standing on one leg — explained that a post-mortem was a legal requirement in the case of sudden death or accident.

She repeated the Doctor's suggestion about getting the vet round, a suggestion Mrs Cassidy poo-pooed immediately, insisting there was nothing about horse behaviour a vet could tell her. If they were to go and see Chanter together now, then she could do a far better job, she said.

Casey had pretty quickly understood that she was talking to a woman who was used to being in charge and who was very rarely gainsaid. She wanted to say that, actually, she'd prefer to take the advice of the vet — but what would her reason be? Mainly to show this woman that if anyone was in charge here, it was her, Detective

Inspector Casey Clunes of the Brock-haven Police.

What was wrong in letting Emma Cassidy win? This wasn't about her ego. It was simply about getting the answer to a question. And if this woman she'd taken an instant dislike to knew the answers, then why involve a third party?

'Okay,' she said. 'Let's go.'

★   ★   ★

Casey and Gail were in Gail's SUV, heading back to the station. With uniform on guard and Kelly now safe in the care of an anxious mum who'd come to pick her up and whisk her off home, there was little else for them to do.

'Tell me again why we're driving to work instead of going straight home to enjoy the rest of our day off?' Casey said.

'Because we're nuts?'

The truth was less light-hearted. Her place of work could sometimes be a refuge. Right now, she needed time and space away from her family to rinse from her mind today's episode. Only then would she feel she could get back to normal and perhaps begin to think about popping down to the beach to look for Dom and the kids to join them in their shell hunt. She was pretty certain Gail felt the same as she did but, like herself, would rather make a joke of it.

En route, she repeated what she'd learned about Chanter. He was a rescue horse who'd been in a bad state when he first came to the stables. Now though, he let anybody ride him. Even children who'd never ridden before. As for Emma Cassidy herself, although Casey hadn't much warmed to her as a person, she couldn't help admiring the woman's horse-training skills.

Gail reminded her that Chanter had just kicked down a stable door and trampled some poor girl to death. Some skills, she said. She left out the bit about what he'd almost done to her and Finlay.

★   ★   ★

Casey spotted Colin Janner all alone at a big table, tucking into a plate of chips and

88

a pie. He looked tired, like a man who'd done a long night shift on desk duty. She went over to join him while Gail went to get the coffees.

'Thought you two were off duty for a couple of days?' he said.

Quickly, Casey explained the events of the morning. By the time she'd finished, Gail was back with some much-needed coffee and biscuits.

'Where was this again?' he said.

'Sycamore Stables,' Casey said. 'It's out by Oakham Manor.'

Colin put his fork down. He appeared to be thinking hard.

'And it was a young woman's body you found, you say?'

'Only twenty-one, according to the other girl who worked there.'

'Too soon to know the time of death, I suppose?'

Casey explained that there would have to be an autopsy, of course, but that it had been more or less 10.30 when they'd arrived and she didn't think they'd been there more than twenty minutes when the horse had come storming out of its stable.

'And you're definitely calling it an accident, are you?'

'What do you mean?' Gail and Casey spoke in unison.

'Couple of officers brought a lad in last night. Cameron Finch. Drunk as a skunk. Picked up in town for being abusive to anyone and everyone. I charged him and between three of us we threw him in the cells to sober up. I had the pleasure of his company for most of the night. Crying like a baby, he was. Calling out some girl's name who'd dumped him. The reason for him going on a bender, he said. Sadie, Sadie, all night long on and off. God, he was annoying.'

Casey and Gail glanced at each other.

'You're sure that's the name he called out?' Casey said.

'Definitely. I remember it clearly. It's my mother-in-law's name, you see. You don't hear it so much nowadays, do you?' Colin picked up his mug of half-drunk tea and took a noisy slurp. 'Said he was a farrier. That's how he met his girlfriend. Or his ex. At some stables or other.' Another slurp of tea. 'They can be very chatty when they've had a drink.'

'Is he still in the cell?' Casey asked, hopefully.

Her hopes were soon dashed. Colin had released him — badly hungover — at six, whereupon he'd made a phone call to a friend to come and collect him.

'You don't think we may have got this wrong?' Gail said. 'That this wasn't an accident after all?'

Casey didn't know how to reply. So many questions flashed through her mind, toppling over each other in their urgency to be addressed.

What if this boy — this Cameron Finch — had got his friend to drive him all the way to Sycamore Stables, where he'd been dropped off? And what if he'd then made his way to the stable yard where he knew his ex-girlfriend would be working the early shift and, after some sort of confrontation, murdered her?

Then there was the horse. What if it turned out it that Chanter was just a scapegoat and had had nothing to do with Sadie's death at all? 'I've known horses spooked by a paper bag floating by,'

Emma Cassidy had told her. Maybe it had been something like that, something out of the blue that had set the horse off and Sadie Cassidy was already dead? Maybe she'd been lying in that stable just feet away from him and had been dead for hours? Overnight, even!

Then Casey was struck by another thought. Sinking her head into her hands, she let out a long groan of despair. If the stable was a crime scene, and not the scene of an accident as they'd first thought, then she shouldn't have allowed anyone in unless they were gowned up. One glance at Gail and she knew she was thinking just the same.

'You can't possibly have known, Casey.' Gail's words reached her from a distance. At least she'd got uniform round to keep the public at bay, and quickly too, she said. Besides, where would it get her, heaping all this blame onto herself?

Gail's words took away some of the sting. What she needed to do now was to pull herself together and earn her rank. There was no time for self-pity. Time was of the essence. They were going to have to search Finch's house and van before he managed to get rid of any incriminating evidence. But for that they needed a warrant.

'I know his address,' Colin said, springing up. 'I'll sort it. And you'll need a couple of officers to do the search.'

Gail volunteered to get in touch with the two uniform down at the stables and bring them up to speed, then to organise a SOCO team to do a thorough search of the stable.

'Do you want to go with them?' she asked Casey.

Casey shook her head. The pleasure would be all Gail's, she said. What she wanted, more than anything, was to get a closer look at Cameron Finch. In fact, she couldn't wait.

★   ★   ★

They'd run a check on Finch before setting out. Nineteen years old, so younger than Sadie by a couple of years. Lived with his mother in Hokham, which was more a hamlet than a village, a couple of miles inland. No previous.

Cameron Finch's mother answered the door. When she saw the posse of police officers on the doorstep, she took a step back. Casey introduced herself and the two officers who accompanied her. They needed to speak to Cameron and to conduct a thorough search of the property, she said. And before Mrs Finch started making difficulties about wanting to see a warrant, there was one on the way.

Once inside, she ordered Toni to stay with Mrs Finch and not let her out of her sight until Casey came back downstairs.

'You come with me, Trev,' she said to the other officer. 'I've heard our boy's handy with his fists.'

Trev Jackson was six foot two and built like the proverbial. She wouldn't fancy Finch's chances against Trev. Not with the hangover he would surely still have.

It was a short distance from the bottom of the stairs to the landing. Casey was faced with three doors. One, the bathroom, was ajar. She had to make a choice between the other two. And she was right first time.

'In we go,' she muttered to her companion.

As soon as she opened it a tiny crack, she was greeted by a fetid mix of smells — unwashed male body mixed with stale alcohol. She'd smelled worse things, she supposed, wrinkling her nose as she pushed the door open.

If Cameron Finch had a guilty conscience, it didn't seem to be interfering with his ability to sleep. The duvet beneath which he slept rose and fell with each breath, and every now and then he emitted a gentle snore. Marching up to the bed, Trev yanked the duvet off, revealing the sleeping Cameron, naked as the day he was born.

'Very nice,' Casey said. 'Now put him back. I'm a married woman.'

With a grin, Trev obliged. Casey's eyes fell immediately upon a heap of tangled clothes at the side of the bed. Giving the order to Trev to bag them, Casey decided it was time to rouse Sleeping Beauty.

It took the two of them in the end. When finally he opened his eyes, he

stared at them, blearily and uncompre-
hendingly at first.

'Police,' she said. 'Get dressed. You're
coming with me to the station.'

From being half asleep he was now
suddenly wide awake.

'Does the name Sadie Warren mean
anything to you?' Casey said, watching
him closely.

She saw pain on his face, a broken
heart reflected in his eyes. Men killed for
less.

'Of course it does. She was my
girlfriend. Until yesterday.'

'And what happened yesterday, Cameron?'

'You know what happened,' he said.
'I had a skinful. Started a fight. Got
arrested.'

'Anything else?'

He stared at the floor, desolate once
more. 'Sadie,' he began. 'She . . . '

'I wouldn't say any more just yet, lad,'
Trev said. 'Leave it for the station.'

Casey's phone suddenly burst into life.
When she fished it out of her pocket she
saw it was Gail.

'You need to get dressed immediately,' she said.

Cameron's eyes widened like saucers. He was obviously the modest kind. It was almost sweet. She told him she had to take the phone call outside, so he needn't worry about her being there. P.C. Jackson wouldn't peep either, she assured him. As if on cue, Trev turned his back deliberately, before wandering over to the window to ponder the view.

Once outside Casey turned her attention to the phone call.

'Gail,' she said. 'What's up?'

The heavy silence went for so long that Casey began to wonder if they'd been cut off. Finally, Gail spoke. She didn't know if she could bring herself to say what she knew she must, she said.

'For heaven's sake, Gail,' said Casey. 'Just get on with it.'

Gail swore it wasn't the fault of the officers on guard, that they'd been corralled into it, and that Casey herself had said how domineering Emma Cassidy was, and how it would it take a determined person to stand up to her . . .

'And those two guys — well, they just weren't man enough.'

By now Casey's head was reeling. 'What have they done? Please, just spit it out. I'm losing the will to live here,' she said.

So Gail told her. When they'd arrived at the riding school, there had been no sign of the police officers at the entrance, just a sign saying the school was closed and that all enquiries should be made to the owner. So they'd headed for the stable block with all their equipment and everything, ready to start work.

'And there they were,' Gail said. 'Hard at work. They'd already piled up all the bits of door the horse had kicked in. When we arrived they were sweeping out the stable, under the gimlet eye of Mrs Cassidy.'

'They what?' Casey couldn't believe what she was hearing.

'I know,' Gail said. 'I'm sorry. It looks like the crime scene has been totally compromised. What do we do now?'

* * *

It was probably a stupid idea to think she could salvage something from the situation, but Casey was the ultimate optimist. So, five minutes after she'd summoned another police officer to take over the house search, she jumped in her car, leaving Cameron Finch in the capable hands of Toni and Trev, whose orders were to transport him to the station as soon as their colleague arrived. Once there, they were to let Finch stew for a couple of hours, to wait for his brief and Casey's return.

A much better idea was to call Dom, who would no doubt be wondering for how much longer he was expected to remain in sole charge of Finlay and Molly. Thank God for hands-free phones!

'You're ringing to tell me you won't be coming home for a while, right?'

Dom had to shout to be heard above the shrieking children, who were clearly having a rare old time — although she couldn't vouch for Dom on that score, who sounded nothing if not harassed.

'I'm sorry,' she said. 'I have to go back to the stables.'

'I didn't know you'd left.'

'No, of course not,' she said. 'It's all got a bit complicated.'

She waited for him to say that it always did, but instead he told her that it had got a bit complicated his end too. Her first reaction was concern. She hoped Finlay hadn't had a wobble about his earlier experience, she said.

Dom's reply came back muffled. By the sound of things they were outside. There was a noise competition going on between a barking dog and the two shrieking children, and from where she sat there was no clear winner.

'I can't hear you properly,' she said.

There it was again, *woof-woof-woof*. Damn dog! She was under the impression that dogs weren't allowed on the beach. That was where he'd said they were going, wasn't it?

'Where are you all?' she said.

'What?'

She repeated the question but still couldn't make out his reply. But she was almost at her destination now and had no time to pursue the conversation.

'Listen, love, I'll call you later, okay?' she said.

The last thing she heard was another explosion of loud laughter accompanied by one more frenzied outbreak of dog barking. The more she thought about it, the more convinced she was that, compared to Dom, she was getting off lightly today.

★   ★   ★

Casey parked well away from the entrance to the stables. The last thing she wanted was to add even more confusion to the situation by leaving her tyre marks all over the place. She'd also managed to find a couple of plastic bags for her feet in the glove compartment. While she slipped them over her muddy trainers, the phrase 'shutting the stable door after the horse has bolted' occurred to her. Oh, the irony.

Once out in the open, she inhaled the sweet smell of manure again. Over in the paddock, some half a dozen horses grazed, flicking away flies with their tails, oblivious to the day's earlier drama.

She stood for a moment and watched them. People could learn a thing or two from animals, she reflected. Some half lines from a poem she'd learned at school, centuries ago, floated into her head. Something about life not being worth anything much unless we could find time to stand around and do nothing once in a while.

These horses had that skill down to a T. Pity she couldn't stay awhile and cultivate their habit. But she had work to do. It was time to move on, past a series of ramshackle outhouses, past the stark, utilitarian, new stable block that more closely resembled a factory than a home for horses, and past the rather uninspiring riding arena.

What Casey knew about show jumping could be written on the back of a winner's rosette. But the milk crates with poles slung across them at Sycamore Stables and Riding School bore very little resemblance to those magnificent constructions she'd glimpsed elegantly-dressed equestrians sail over, and occasionally crash into, on TV.

When she finally arrived at the old stable block, she was met by a lonely figure. Jenn Darwin, the Scene of Crime officer, dressed from head to toe in her white gown, stepped forward to meet her. There was no sign either of Gail or of the two officers she'd put in charge of keeping the public off the land. Casey wondered if Gail had hidden them away somewhere, fearful for their safety once Casey turned up.

Jenn, a young, slightly-built woman in her early thirties, was new to the job, very efficient and rather shy. Her manner made a massive change from other SOCOs Casey had met over the years, who enjoyed nothing more than showing off their far superior knowledge in front of a member of the unscientific community.

'Where are the two donkeys that did this?' Casey asked her, once the hellos were out of the way.

'This' was a pile of wood, consisting of pieces from the broken stable door, neatly laid against the wall alongside a couple of brooms — no doubt used to sweep out Chanter's stall.

'Gail's making them go through the horse's bedding,' Jenn said, her lips briefly twitching. 'One of them suffers from hay fever, apparently. But I doubt she'll be showing him any sympathy.'

'That's my girl,' Casey said. 'I thought she'd gone soft for a minute.'

Jenn smiled again.

'So, how long have they been at it?'

'Ages. There's a lot of hay in that stall. And we might be looking for a needle.'

Metaphors were obviously catching.

'Can we go inside?'

'Be my guest.'

Jenn informed Casey that there would be no need for her to gown up, since she'd been round the walls already, and her team had already left with some samples — though what these would throw up was anyone's guess, given how badly the scene had been compromised. Because of that, she'd also insisted on taking prints and DNA from the two officers and Mrs Cassidy, who had proved a very disobliging participant.

'What did she say?' Casey demanded.

They were inside now. The stall was

bare, apart from one or two grooming instruments on the wall, and a lucky horseshoe that dangled at a comic angle. Not so lucky for someone, in this case.

'Oh, you know. Came the big 'I am'. She shut up when I told her she might well be arrested for disturbing a crime scene.'

Casey already liked Jenn Darwin. She liked her even more with that remark.

'So all we can do now is wait to see what results come back from your lot, and pray that P.C.s Wilkes and Houlder can manage to redeem themselves.'

At that very moment Jenn's phone rang. She pounced on it immediately. Her eyes narrowed as she listened attentively, then a look of triumph passed over her face. It was as if the sun had finally come out of the shade.

'They've found something,' she said. 'They're on their way over.'

★ ★ ★

Casey's hopes had risen when P.C.s Wilkes and Houlder — red-eyed and sneezing, but not daring to complain — had turned up with a mobile phone. Whoever it belonged to, the victim or the culprit, it was bound to contain something of relevance to the case, she reasoned.

But the battery was flat, so nothing could be retrieved until it was recharged. And besides, even if had been fully charged, no one would have been allowed to touch it until it had undergone a thorough examination.

They'd also picked up an empty crisp packet, a bus ticket, last Friday's edition of The Brockhaven Gazette, and a rather crumpled business card. Wilkes and Houlder were clearly taking no chances, this time.

It was the business card that had interested Casey most. 'Equinity' she'd managed to read, squinting through the plastic it had been safely tucked away in. She'd just about been able to make out the outline of a horse's head and some contact details she couldn't read, apart from Sadie's name, which was more prominent. But she'd quickly lost interest.

So what if Sadie Warren did have her own business on the side? It wasn't a crime.

Casey had left for the station then, having dealt with the two officers — very lightly under the circumstances. In fairness to them, she believed them when they said that Emma Cassidy had simply taken over. She was a terrifying cross between Margaret Thatcher and Boadicea, with a touch of Sir Alan Sugar thrown in, they said. She'd had them mucking out before they could come up with a reason why it wasn't a good idea.

Back at the station she hadn't got very far with Cameron Finch either. He'd sat through the interview repeating 'No comment,' to every single question Casey put to him, which was his right of course. There was not a single shred of evidence against him, since the search of his house had produced nothing, and his clothes from the previous day were still with forensics. In the end, they'd let him go without charge, warning him he hadn't seen the last of them.

So it was an exhausted and somewhat downbeat Casey who let herself into the house sometime after eight that night, hoping that whatever Dom had made for dinner was still edible.

The first thing she heard as she opened the front door was a muffled *woof*. Then a wet, black nose appeared from behind the lounge door. There's a saying: if it walks like a duck and quacks like a duck, then it's a duck. Substitute the words 'dog' and 'bark' and what she now had sitting at her feet, gazing up at her expectantly, its pink tongue darting all over the place, was indeed a dog.

Not just any old dog either, but a rather gorgeous spaniel whose coat was the colour of that shiny melted chocolate every Masterchef competitor strove to achieve when it came to pulling off a show-stopping dessert. And as for its eyes — they were the colour of treacle toffee.

'What the . . . ?'

'Mum! We've got a dog!'

Finlay, in his pyjamas, arrived in the hall moments after the dog had decided to introduce itself. The little boy's face shone with ecstasy, as he and the equally

108

ecstatic hound fell into each other's embrace.

Dom, who'd been observing all this from behind the living room door, looked rather more reserved when he finally showed his face.

'It's not what you're thinking, Casey,' Dom said. 'And Finlay,' he added, turning to his son, 'remember what I said? We're only looking after the dog until the owner claims him.'

'Look, can I take my coat off?' Casey demanded. 'And is there anything to eat? Otherwise I might just pass out.'

★   ★   ★

Over a plate of scrambled eggs on toast which Dom hastily threw together, amid apologies for the absence of the sausages he'd earmarked for today's dinner because they'd ended up inside the dog, he explained why they'd suddenly found themselves in possession of a rather lively eighteen-month-old spaniel.

'We found him on the beach,' he said. 'He just sort of started hanging out with us and when we left he tagged along. To be honest, I didn't really notice him until we got to the High Street. I had my hands full with Finlay and Molly.'

'He's called Treacle,' Finlay said. ' 'Cos of his eyes.'

'Steady on, Finlay. We don't know what his name is. This dog belongs to someone else, and when we discover who that someone else is then we're going to have to give him back.'

Finlay's mouth began to turn down, his cheeks grew red and his eyes started to glisten. The signs were there. Casey and Dom exchanged knowing glances, recognizing them immediately. Finlay was about to go into total meltdown.

'A dog should have a collar,' Finlay said. 'Anyone who doesn't put a collar on their dog doesn't deserve to keep him. They should be sent to prison.'

Finlay had a rather black and white view of justice.

'Calm down, Finlay,' Casey said. 'If you get upset in front of the dog it will pick it up immediately and get upset too. Dogs are very sensitive creatures.'

Her words did the trick. Finlay calmed down immediately and didn't even put up much of a fight when Dom told him in no uncertain terms that the dog would not be allowed to sleep at the foot of his bed.

'So what exactly have you done to find out who this dog belongs to?' Casey wanted to know, once Finlay had finally been persuaded to say goodnight to the dog he insisted on calling Treacle.

They were in the lounge, enjoying a much-needed glass of wine. The dog lay at Dom's feet as if he was his rightful master, and he was exactly where he belonged. Every now and then he cocked his head this way and that, as if he knew he was the one under discussion.

Dom told her that he'd gone on Facebook, where Brockhaven had a page of its own. He'd posted a picture of the dog and asked its owner to get in touch. Failing that, if anyone knew the dog and who it belonged to, could they make contact in a private message?

'You've checked your messages, presumably?' Casey said. It was gone ten and she'd been home a while now. So far he'd

111

gone nowhere near his laptop.

'No, not yet.'

She watched him swirl his wine around his glass. Finlay did the same thing when he was evading a question. With milk or lemonade, of course, not wine. But the message was the same.

'You don't want anyone to claim him, do you?' Casey heaved herself out of her chair, headed for Dom's study, and returned with his laptop.

'Here,' she said. 'Do it now. If the owner's got in touch with you then you need to ring them and tell them to come and collect their property right away.'

'But what will Finlay say in the morning?'

There were two pairs of mournful eyes watching her now. She felt such a heel.

'We'll cross that bridge when we get to it,' she said.

It had been a day for clichés.

★ ★ ★

Casey was hollow-eyed and miserable next morning. Gail, looking bright, breezy

112

and smart in her uniform, commented on it immediately. Casey explained about the dog situation — some of which had already been relayed to her by little Molly, who'd been as besotted by the dog as Finlay — and Dom. Dom'd been gutted when he saw the message in his inbox claiming Oscar the dog. To prove it, the writer of the message — Sal Waller — sent a picture of the two of them together. There was no mistaking that the dog in the picture was definitely the one Finlay had christened Treacle.

'The owner turned up around midnight,' Casey explained. 'Apparently he'd slipped his collar and she'd been looking for him ever since.'

Except, it turned out, the dog wasn't really hers. It belonged to her boyfriend, who wasn't able to look after it at the moment as he was working abroad, so she was looking after it instead.

Finlay, of course, had been broken-hearted when he'd woken up to find his new four-legged friend was no longer in the house. This time, with nothing to put the brakes on his emotions, he'd had a full-on tantrum.

'I feel awful coming to work and leaving him so upset,' Casey said, sipping the coffee Gail had so thoughtfully put in her front of her.

'Well, I've got a bit of news that might make you feel better,' Gail said. 'The PM report on Sadie came through. Estimated time of death between midnight and nine a.m. Blunt force trauma. And like the GP said, inter-cranial bleeding.'

'In that case, we need to speak to Cameron Finch again,' Casey said. 'He left the cell here at six yesterday morning. He needs to explain where he went then.'

Gail said they were already onto it.

'Jenn's been on the phone asking for you, too,' she said. 'Said she had some news on the mobile phone the lads found.'

Casey smiled for the first time that morning. It looked like they might be making headway at last. Taking her coffee with her, she headed for her office and got straight back to Jenn, who answered immediately.

'I think I can hazard a guess about

what spooked your horse,' Jenn said. 'Sadie Warren's phone rang three times in succession yesterday morning. 10.45, 10.46 and 10.47. The ring tone was set to some ghastly rap tune with the kind of lyrics that would make your mother blush. A cacophony like that could easily make a horse bolt.'

Perhaps it was possible, Casey agreed, remembering what Emma Cassidy had told her about even the most placid of horses being spooked by ridiculous things. Who'd made the call, she wanted to know.

'Someone called Kelly. No message the first and second times, but an irate, 'Where the hell are you?' the final time.'

That made sense too. Kelly was Sadie's co-worker, Casey explained.

'What about the other callers?' she added.

Jenn reeled them off. The period of time that most interested her was the final twenty-four hours of Sadie's life. There were a couple of dozen calls in all during that time.

'Popular girl,' Casey remarked.

'Well, sixteen of them were from Cameron Finch. I've instructed her mobile network provider to send the WAV files over to you. There'll probably be about four of them,' Jenn said. 'I'm warning you, you might need to cancel lunch.'

'You've listened already, I'm guessing?'

Jenn laughed. Actually she'd given up after the first half dozen. They were all a bit samey, she'd said. But then again, she wasn't the detective.

Casey's landline suddenly burst into life. Bidding Jenn a hasty goodbye — although not before thanking her for her work — she answered it. It was a P.C. Colin Fox. The name didn't ring a bell.

'I'm from Devden,' he said. 'I went out with another officer to see the parents of Sadie Warren yesterday afternoon, to inform them of their daughter's death.'

'That can't have been easy,' she said.

'It never is, usually, is it?' he said. 'But this time — well. Between you and me, I didn't get the response I anticipated.'

It was the lack of emotion her parents displayed that surprised him, he said.

'They were just so matter-of-fact about the news,' he said. 'It was as if I was making them a visit to say I'd found their car abandoned in a ditch somewhere. Thanked me for calling and did I want a cup of tea?'

'Surely not?'

Pretty well, he said. But the oddest thing had been when Mrs Warren had shown them to the door.

'She told me that she'd often imagined getting a visit from the police about Sadie and so she hadn't been at all surprised to see the car outside her door,' he said. 'But she'd never expected to hear her daughter had had an accident with a horse. Being as how she was so good with them, like.'

He paused. Casey had been doodling on her notebook all the while he spoke, wondering where all this was leading and when exactly he was going to get to the point.

'And then she said this. She said, 'Funny, when I saw your car draw up today, I was fully expecting you to knock on my door and tell me my daughter had been murdered.''

* * *

Casey rubbed her eyes and yawned. Thank God *that* was over. There had been sixteen messages from Cameron Finch to Sadie Warren between seven p.m. and seven a.m. Most of them were clustered around the hour between ten and eleven, at which point, presumably, he was picked up by the police and brought back to the station to sober up in a cell overnight.

They'd started off coherently enough. Initially there was shock and disbelief but as the night progressed his speech grew more slurred and he sounded more and more angry. There was a lot of name-calling and a great deal of colourful language, alternating with desperate drunken pleas for Sadie to reconsider her decision. All innocent stuff, given the circumstances. Until she came to the final message, delivered just after he was let out of his cell, at 06.07 in the morning.

It said simply, 'I know where you'll be so I'm coming over.' Was there a threat lurking in those words? She knew straightaway how a clever solicitor would react if she suggested as much. She was twisting Finch's words, reading something into them that didn't exist. Finding him guilty just because he was a working class boy who lacked eloquence. Casey had heard it all before, and more too.

Her thoughts turned to Mrs Warren, and what she'd said to P.C. Fox when he'd delivered the news of her daughter's death. What was it about Sadie Warren that might provoke her own mother to say she wasn't surprised her daughter had been murdered?

The face of her own son came into her mind. Finlay — who this morning had snubbed her deliberately as she'd left the house — was still furious with her for allowing someone to take 'Treacle' away.

Naturally, she worried about him from time to time. What mother didn't worry about her children? But the thought that one day someone might want to murder him — and that if they had, he'd probably been asking for it — had never once crossed her mind even in her worst nightmares!

Casey was going to have to pay the Warrens a visit and find out more about their little girl. She was going to need to speak to Kelly, and Emma Cassidy too, since they'd worked with Sadie and would have had some insight into her character. But for now, she'd make a start with Cameron Finch, who'd presumably known her better than most people.

*   *   *

'You must have been very upset when Sadie broke off your relationship.' Casey sat across the table from Cameron Finch in the tiny, airless, interview room. He looked tired, and slightly bewildered, she thought. 'Eighteen months is a long time to be with someone. Tell me how you met.'

Finch stared at his hands. They were rather large hands, the palms broad, yet his fingers were short and stubby and his nails, which he bit, were grimy.

'Through work,' he said. 'I shoe the horses for Mrs Cassidy. Sadie had just started working there as a groom. We got talking and, you know, just clicked.'

Casey moved onto the messages he'd sent Sadie, passing over to him the pages and pages of transcript. He seemed a little embarrassed by the amount of black ink his words took up on the page.

It was all on account of the drink, he said, sheepishly. He wasn't used to it and he'd started too soon and drank too quickly. It'd put him in a rage, he added, a phrase that drew a sharp intake of breath and a warning glance from his solicitor.

'Why did you ring her again in the morning?' Casey said.

'She had something of mine I needed back,' he said. 'I didn't see why she should keep it. She's had enough off of me.'

'Like what, exactly?'

'Money, for one thing,' he said. 'She had an idea for a business. Needed money for the outlay. The bank was no good for it. So she asked this sucker here. It must have been a disappointment when she realised I didn't have any more spare cash to give her.'

Casey remembered the business card found at the scene. Equinity. When Casey asked if he knew the nature of her business idea, Finch was vague.

'It changed every week,' he said. 'But it was always something to do with horses.'

'You don't seem very upset about what happened to her, considering you'd been in a relationship with her, Cameron,' Casey said, moving on.

'It ain't sunk in yet,' he said.

That could be true, of course.

'So, what else did she have of yours?'

Finch said that he'd left his tools at the stables. He'd had another job to go to once he'd gone home, had a sleep and a shower. But without his tools he couldn't make a start on it.

As it happened, he grumbled, he hadn't made it to the job anyway, since 'you lot' had turned up and dragged him out of bed. Casey let him complain a bit more about the length of time it had taken to summon a brief, and for his interview to start, and how he'd probably lost the contract now anyway, because when the guy rang his house to ask where he was, his daft mother had told him that he was helping the police with their enquiries.

But, he insisted, he never actually followed up his phone call to Sadie with a visit. Once his mate had driven him about a mile, he'd decided he couldn't face her, looking and feeling as rough as he did. He'd asked his mate to drop him off at home instead, which he had.

Cameron Finch's solicitor spoke up for the first time. 'Unless you're planning to charge my client, then I really think you need to let him go,' he said. 'There still isn't one scrap of evidence that puts Mr Finch at the scene of the murder.'

Unfortunately, there wasn't a scrap of evidence at the crime scene to put anyone there, let alone Cameron Finch. Not that Casey was about to reveal police incompetence to this guy, who'd think nothing of leaking what she told him to the press. And once they got hold of it, they'd have a field day.

'You're right,' she said. 'You're free to go, Cameron.'

Finch looked momentarily stunned. He turned to his solicitor to check he'd not misheard. The solicitor nodded encouragingly and began to collect his things together.

'Just before you leave, though, Cameron,' she said. 'One: we're still waiting to hear from forensics about the clothes you were wearing on your night out. Two: this friend who picked you up from the station. We'll be checking out your story with him. And three: those tools you said you'd left behind at the stables. We'll be checking out their existence too.'

That damn solicitor wasn't going to get away with it so easily.

* * *

'I'm really not sure that's a good idea, Dom.'

Casey was at the wheel of her car, having programmed the satnav to deliver her safely to Briar Drive, Devden, where Mr and Mrs Warren lived at number sixteen.

Her conscience had been pricking her ever since she'd left home this morning to come to work. Just a quick call, to see how Finlay is, was what she'd told herself. Now, though, she was on the verge of a row with Dom, who was behaving like just the sort of indulgent parent they'd always been united in scoffing at.

'I know he's upset about not being allowed to keep the dog,' she said. 'But we can't just turn round and buy him a replacement.'

Wouldn't that just be teaching him he could get anything he wanted if he sulked for long enough? she added.

'You can't always get what you want, Dom,' she said. 'As somebody once famously sang.'

She'd hoped to inject some levity into the conversation, but the prolonged silence on the other end of the line suggested she'd failed abysmally.

'It's all right for you,' Dom finally spoke. 'You don't have to endure his unhappy little face.'

'I'm on a case, Dom. I can't just drop it because my child's feeling hard done by. Can't you both go out somewhere and take his mind off it?'

Another silence. Then, 'It's not just him though.'

'What do you mean?'

Only that the more he thought about it, the more certain he was that the woman who'd turned up to claim Treacle — or Oscar, or whatever his name was — hadn't been terribly happy about it. Not only that, but he was certain the feeling was mutual. The dog had seemed equally reluctant to leave with her.

'You're not suggesting she mistreats him, surely?'

'No, not at all. Just that . . . Well, the dog seemed more of a burden than a beloved companion.'

Casey remembered the woman mentioning it was actually her boyfriend's dog, not hers. Perhaps Dom was right, and she'd been unwillingly coerced into looking after him.

'The look in that dog's eyes when he had to say goodbye. He really didn't want to go.'

There was a word, wasn't there, for attaching human feelings to animals? Dom, the writer and journalist, would surely know what it was.

'You'll say I'm just anthropomorphiz-ing.'

Of course he did.

'I wouldn't,' she said, 'because it's not an easy word to say.'

'I'm being serious, Casey. Why do you always have to make light of things?'

'I'm sorry. I don't want to row. Look, I'm at my destination now. Can we leave it until I get home?'

'Do I have a choice?'

He was still mad at her. Please, please do not go out and get a dog in my absence, she fervently prayed, as she switched off the engine. She wouldn't have put it past him.

★   ★   ★

The first thing that struck Casey about the Warrens house was its extreme tidiness. What few books they possessed were lined up in a neat row on the single bookshelf in their living room. Cushions were plumped, fruit was arranged into a neat pyramid, and there wasn't a dirty cup or a crumpled newspaper in sight. It was quite the most sterile environment Casey had ever seen. The second thing she noticed was that there was not a single photograph of Sadie on view.

Mrs Warren, as neat as her house, repeatedly either patted her hair to check it was perfectly in place, or picked invisible threads of cotton off her clothes. All this while keeping up a constant stream of conversation and setting out the tea things — because of course, Casey *must* have a cup of tea after her drive!

She was sorry Mr Warren wasn't here, the patter continued, but he'd been having trouble with a wisdom tooth, and when she'd rung the dentist on his behalf — men never could do these things for themselves could they? — they'd said they had a cancellation so she'd sent him off to the surgery immediately.

Finally, with the tea poured and Mrs Warren sitting down at last, Casey took the bull by the horns and spoke the words she'd practiced in her head as she'd stood at the front door while waiting for someone to open it.

'I'm afraid we don't think your daughter's death was an accident after all, Mrs Warren. We believe she was murdered.'

Mrs Warren didn't flinch. She simply took a sip of her tea before replacing the cup back in its saucer with a delicate movement of her fingers.

'It must be a shock for you,' Casey said, making it sound more like a question than an expression of sympathy. She thought she could hear someone coming into the house. Mr Warren back from his trip to the dentist, she presumed. If Mrs Warren had heard him, she gave no sign.

'You'd think so, wouldn't you,' Mrs Warren said. 'But the truth is — and I'm sorry to have to say this, and about how it must sound — my daughter wasn't a very nice person.'

Well, she hadn't expected her to be quite so forthright!

'Right from being a child she was selfish, thoughtless and manipulative,' she continued. 'God knows I've felt like killing her myself over the years often enough.'

'Deirdre, how can you say that about your own child?'

Casey glanced up. Mr Warren stood at the door, red-faced and swollen-jawed, his speech slurred.

'Because you know I'm right, Geoff,' she said. 'Just remember what she's done to your health over the years. Ruined it, she has.'

She revealed that her husband had had two minor heart attacks in the last couple of years, brought on, she said, over money worries.

'The only time we ever saw her was when she wanted money,' she went on.

'Deirdre. Please. She was our daughter, in spite of everything.'

'And we were her parents. She didn't lift a finger to help me when you had your first heart attack and I was still struggling to get over my op. Then, when I rang her to tell her about the second and asked her if she could come home and lend a hand, she said she was too busy trying to set up this business of hers.'

'Maybe she was.'

Mrs Warren gave her husband a look of scorn. 'Business! It was all play-acting, if you ask me. She was just the same as a girl. Ideas above her station, she had.'

There were tears in Mrs Warren's eyes now. However well she'd thought she'd convinced herself that she'd turned her back on her daughter, Casey wasn't convinced she was totally without feelings for her. Unless she was simply crying for herself and her ill luck in having given birth to such an inconsiderate child.

'When was the last time she visited?' Casey wanted to know.

'A couple of weeks ago, wasn't it, Geoff?'

Mrs Warren nodded. She'd caused a big scene, apparently, because for the first time her father had stood up to her. When he'd told her they couldn't lend her another penny, she'd become hysterical, accusing them both of wrecking her business before she could even get it off the ground, he said. And then Mrs Warren chimed in.

'I sent her packing. I could see she was making Geoff ill again. I told her I wanted her to leave and I never wanted to see her again.' Now she was in full floods of tears. 'But I didn't mean this. I swear I didn't mean this.'

*   *   *

A parent's guilt was a dreadful, all-consuming thing, Casey mused, as she drove back towards Brockhaven. She'd found Mrs Warren an unsympathetic character at first, but now she could only feel sorry for her.

She had a sneaking admiration for her too, because she'd faced up to some difficult feelings towards her child. Feelings that society regarded as the last taboo. Blood was thicker than water, so the saying went. A convenient proverb to be trotted out when the truth was just too hard to bear, perhaps.

Back in the car, Casey checked her messages. Nothing from Dom, which suggested he was still sulking. One from Jenn, to say that the tests on Cameron Finch's clothes had proved inconclusive, which told her absolutely nothing. The other two were more interesting.

A couple of officers had, on her orders, been dispatched to the stables to look for Finch's toolbox. And it appeared he'd been telling the truth. The toolbox was there, all right, hiding away on the top shelf of the tack room.

One of the other girls who worked there — Kelly, Casey guessed — had shown them where to look. But when they'd opened it they'd discovered that — according to the girl, anyway — one of the farrier's tools was missing.

And then there was the last message. This one was from Gail, a voicemail.

'You might be interested in this, Casey,' it said. 'Clarke. Finch's mate. He picked Finch up all right. But he didn't take him home. Swore he dropped him just half a mile away from the stables, at Finch's suggestion. Finch said he needed to get his head together before he went to talk to Sadie.'

As she was listening and wondering what to make of this new piece of information, another message pinged through. Gail again. She was texting from outside Finch's house, having spoken to his mum. According to Mrs Finch, Cameron had definitely been home before six-thirty. She'd been in bed but hadn't been able to sleep. Never could apparently until he was home, even though he was a grown man. She remembered glancing at the clock and noticing the time.

Casey's head was spinning. So many pieces in the jigsaw, but so far nothing fitted. Who was telling the truth? Finch, Finch's mother, or Daniel, his mate?

Something else was bugging her, and had been for a while now. It was to do with Emma Cassidy, who hadn't been around when Sadie Warren's body had been discovered.

She remembered Gail telling her that Sycamore Stables was a bit of a dump. She'd seen evidence of that with her own eyes. Gail had also said that at one time the owner had had aspirations for the place. Odd, then, that on the first morning of a busy half term week, she'd decided to go off on a run and leave the riding school in the hands of her two young grooms, instead of remaining on the premises to make sure everything ran smoothly.

Then there was the business of cleaning out the stables. Why had Emma Cassidy been so insistent that the two officers cleaned up the stall after the horse had bolted? The obvious answer was that there was something in that stall that she'd wanted to make disappear.

But a much more unsettling feeling was beginning to creep over Casey. She'd been so cross with those officers when she'd discovered how thoughtlessly they'd trampled over the scene of the crime.

But she'd hardly done any better herself. She thought back to the verbal tussle she'd had with Emma Cassidy on that morning. Casey had wanted to call the vet, on the advice of the doctor. But the owner of the stables had pooh-poohed the idea, saying there was nothing a vet could tell her about her own horse. In the end, Casey had relented, agreeing to accompany Mrs Cassidy to the new stall where Chanter had been rehoused so she could check him out.

On the way there, Mrs Cassidy had asked if she might pop in and look at what damage Chanter had caused in his old stall. Casey had thought nothing of it. Why should she have? Back then, she'd thought it was an accident, just as those two luckless police officers had.

How long had she left the woman alone in there while she'd stood outside admiring the view? A minute? Two minutes? Three? She didn't know for sure. But long enough, perhaps, for Emma Cassidy to remove a vital piece of evidence that might implicate her in a murder.

★   ★   ★

Emma Cassidy, dressed in running clothes again, looked none too pleased to find a Detective Sergeant on her doorstep at three in the afternoon.

'Mrs Cassidy! On your way out?' Casey smiled pleasantly.

'I've just got in, actually. Isn't it obvious?'

Emma Cassidy's limp-haired, sweat-slicked appearance hadn't for one second

136

escaped Casey. But she was happy to play along with the woman's interpretation of her as the female version of a bumbling Lestrade.

'You won't mind me stepping inside then, so I can ask you a few questions?'

'I don't suppose I have much choice, do I?'

Casey followed Emma into the little kitchen-cum-office she remembered from her first visit. There it was again, that smell of damp floor mops. The same cloudy water in the vase housing those dead flowers. Emma Cassidy clearly kept her stables in better condition than her own home. Not that Casey would ever judge another woman on the state of her kitchen floor.

'So, what do you want then?'

'What was your relationship with Sadie Warren, Emma?'

For a split second, Emma was caught off balance. Almost immediately, she recovered her usual mask of composure.

'You think I killed her, don't you? You really must be desperate!'

'Just answer the question, Emma.'

Emma strolled over to the sink and ran

the cold water tap for a long time. After testing it with her finger and finding the temperature to her liking, she took a glass from the draining board and filled it to the brim. She didn't speak until she'd drained its entire contents. Oh, how this woman loved to take control!

'OK. I'll tell you.' She rinsed the glass, replaced it on the draining board and wiped her mouth with the back of her hand.

She didn't like Sadie Warren, she said. Although initially, she'd liked her very much. The girl knew horses and seemed to love them, and the feeling was mutual. The clients liked her too. She was pretty, smart, a hard worker and always turned up on time.

'But then I found out she had a bit of a sideline . . . '

According to Emma Cassidy, Sadie had set herself up in her own private business: grooming horses other than those that belonged to the stables. But she was doing it with Emma's tools, often in Emma's time and — even more cheekily — on Emma's premises, for which privilege she paid no rent. Casey remembered the business card found on the stable floor — Equinity.

She'd caught her at it only two days before she was murdered, she said. Gave her a week's notice. She would have sacked her on the spot, but that would have left them understaffed. She'd already had to let one girl go for pilfering, and she couldn't afford to be without another, particularly with the half term week coming up. Normally, she would have been putting in a full day at the stables herself. But she had the marathon to train for.

A lot of money was involved in her run, apparently, with every penny going to a local horse charity. It might have been cynical of Casey to think so, but she'd have put big bucks on the fact that Sycamore Stables would benefit from all the free publicity just as much as the charity would benefit from the money she raised. Emma Cassidy hadn't exactly struck her as the type to do something out of the goodness of her heart.

'So that's what I think of Sadie

Warren,' Emma concluded. 'She was a freeloader. But I didn't kill her.'

'In that case, I'm sure you won't mind if a couple of my officers have a good look round the premises,' said Casey.

Hadn't they done that already, Emma wanted to know. Although tempted, Casey quelled the urge to bring up Emma's part in the validity of that previous search.

'We've searched the stables,' she said. 'We haven't yet conducted a search here in your house.'

Emma widened her eyes. 'My house? Are you serious? What do you think I'm hiding here? The murder weapon?'

Was she really so innocent that she could make jokes about her culpability? Or was this just another one of her smart moves, like turning the stables over before any evidence could be discovered? There was a sudden knock at the door.

'That'll be my guys already.' Casey hoped they'd sent some more reliable officers than the last lot.

When she opened the door she was greeted by three officers, one male and two female. Also standing there was a whey-faced Kelly, who was wondering if she might have a word with the Inspector, one of the officers said.

Casey, keen to find out what Kelly had to say, issued her instructions to the officers as quickly as she could. Under no circumstances was Mrs Cassidy to be left alone, she finished by saying.

'What if she kicks off?' the male officer said.

Casey could hear her already, issuing accusations of police interference. Given Emma Cassidy's temperament, it wouldn't take much perceived provocation before the small gusts of indignation already beginning to erupt from her very quickly escalated into a firestorm.

'Just arrest her,' Casey said, over her shoulder, as she stepped outside.

★   ★   ★

Casey had been slightly uneasy at first, when Kelly suggested Silver's stable for a meeting place. But Kelly reassured her that he was the gentlest of creatures.

141

Casey needn't worry that this horse would bolt like Chanter had done. And once she was introduced to the horse, who lifted his head only briefly to peep shyly with huge brown eyes through a lock of hair, before lowering them indifferently once he'd checked Casey out, she immediately relaxed.

'So, what is it you want to speak to me about, Kelly?' Casey said.

'Thing is,' Kelly said, the words tumbling out in a rush, 'Lily Clarke wasn't the one responsible for stealing those things.'

It took a moment for Casey to realise Kelly was referring to the same groom Emma Cassidy had told her about only a few minutes ago. Immediately intrigued, she asked her to explain.

It was a story that had begun within a couple of weeks of Sadie arriving at the stables, Kelly said. Things started to go missing. Money mostly; a customer's leather jacket, a bag containing a brand new pair of designer trainers. Clients left their things hanging around, despite all the warnings that said they were responsible for their own security.

'I knew it was her — Sadie — though I had no proof. Not while it was going on, anyway,' Kelly said.

She was good friends with Lily, she said. They'd gone to school together. Her brother was best man at Lily's wedding. If Lily had been a thief, she'd have seen signs before.

'You said you had no proof that Sadie was the one responsible,' Casey said.

Kelly nodded. She had it now, though, she said. 'She admitted it. Laughed when she told me, too. Of course, by then she'd already wormed her way into Mrs Cassidy's good books, planted a client's watch in Lily's jacket and got her sacked.'

'You didn't go to Mrs Cassidy and tell her what Sadie had told you?'

'I was scared she'd fit me up in some way if I did. There was something that came off her, a kind of . . . I don't know. I've met girls like her at school and I never could stand up to them.'

Kelly put her hand on the horse's flank and stroked it. Silver turned his head towards her and gave a gentle snort of affection. 'I love my job, Inspector,' she said. 'And there aren't that many opportunities to do what I do round these parts.'

Casey considered Kelly's words. There was no doubting that, by universal agreement, Sadie Warren was a nasty piece of work. But was that especially relevant? Girls were murdered all the time and some of them were the sweetest, most innocent things you could imagine. When her phone pinged a message, she saw it was from Gail. Needing time to think, she decided to ignore it for the moment.

And what about Kelly? She only had her word that Sadie had confessed to being the thief — and Sadie was dead. Kelly had been here in the stable yard the morning Casey, Gail and the children had turned up for the riding lesson that never was. Forensics had been vague about the exact time of Sadie's death. She'd had the same opportunity as her boss, and as Cameron Finch, to kill Sadie Warren.

Cameron Finch's toolbox was stored in the tack room and one of his tools was missing. That was a fact. Any one of those three could have removed it and used it.

If so, where was it now? Even if it was found in Emma Cassidy's house, what would that prove? It was open door access there. She'd walked in herself, alongside Kelly, with no barriers standing in their way whatsoever.

God, she was so tired. What she needed was some headspace. A little time to go back over everything she knew, about Sadie and everyone else who might have a motive.

'Have you finished with me now?'

Kelly's question brought Casey back to the present.

'Yes. Thank you. You've been very helpful.'

Though, really, she wasn't at all sure Kelly had done any more than muddy the waters even further.

'Shall I give you Lily's number?'

Ping. There went her phone again. Who was it this time? Dom. More grief about Oscar, the dog, no doubt.

'Sure,' she said, ignoring it for the moment.

Kelly took out her phone, scrawled through her contacts, located Lily's number and read it out.

'Address?' Casey asked, as she transferred it to her own phone.

Lily and her new husband had lived above The Cross Keys in Devden, Kelly said, until she'd lost her job. Last she'd heard, they were back living with Lily's mum and dad, but she didn't know the address.

'When we spoke last she sounded fed up. Dan and her mum don't get on.'

'The old mother-in-law joke,' Casey said, ruefully, before assuring Kelly they'd soon find Lily from the phone number.

Casey watched Kelly mount her bike and cycle away, before finally getting round to checking her inbox. Continuing to ignore Gail's, she went straight to Dom's, which was a photo message.

There was Finlay, grinning like a Cheshire cat, that endearing gap where his two front baby teeth should have been reminding her how quickly her little boy was growing up.

He was crouching on the ground, his arm draped round a little companion. A companion on four legs with a pink tongue and a shiny coat. Oscar!

She punched in Dom's number. He answered immediately. What was going on, she wanted to know?

'I was right,' Dom said, breathless with excitement. 'She didn't want him after all. So she said we could have him.'

Casey was used to people talking in riddles. She worked this one out in no time. But how could Sal Waller give away a dog she was only temporarily looking after, she wanted to know. What would happen when the boyfriend came back?

'There is no boyfriend. She was . . . well, not lying so much as avoiding the truth.'

'And why would she be doing that?'

'Because . . . ' Dom's sigh reached her, long and loud. 'Her boyfriend died a couple of months ago.'

'How awful! I'm sorry.'

'She's still finding it difficult to accept, sometimes.'

Casey could understand that.

'So we've got her dog?'

'Only if you're alright with it.'

Did she have a choice? One more

glance at that photo would give her the answer.

'I'm coming straight home,' she said. 'After I've just checked in at the station.'

'No need to rush,' Dom said. 'We won't miss you. Not now we've got the dog.'

That's what she loved about Dom. He really knew how to make her feel wanted.

*   *   *

The first person Casey bumped into at the station was Gail.

'You got my message then?' Gail said.

'Message? No.'

Fact was, she'd forgotten all about it after she'd spoken to Dom.

'That missing tool. They found it. One of the officers saw you driving off just as they were about to come and tell you,' Gail said. 'They phoned here instead. A clinching block, it's called.'

'A what?'

'It's a small piece of metal with an angled edge. More importantly, Jenn reckons it's a possible murder weapon.

It's with her now and she's very excited about it.'

'And they found it in Emma Cassidy's house?'

According to Gail, Mrs Cassidy had freely admitted picking it up from the stable floor and carrying it back into her house. 'Said she recognised it as one of the farrier's immediately. She'd wondered what it was doing there and would have put it back in Finch's toolbox, but she thought he needed to learn a lesson about looking after his stuff properly,' Gail said.

'You have to admire her nerve. Did you believe her?'

'I kind of do,' Gail said. 'But it's not up to me.'

The clinching block was clean when they'd found it, she said. But just because there was nothing visible to the naked eye, it didn't mean there was nothing there, did it?

'We could pay Jenn a visit, see how she's getting on with it,' Casey said. 'Or we could do this other thing first.'

Briefly, she explained her recent conversation with Kelly. Gail looked extremely interested at the mention of Lily Clarke.

'You're sure that's her surname?' Gail said, when Casey had reached the end.

'Yes. Why?'

'Because Clarke is the surname of the guy who picked Finch up from the cell and drove him to the stables. Or said he had, though Finch denies it, remember.'

'His mum, too,' Casey remembered.

The two women locked eyes.

'Clarke knew Sadie was responsible for getting his missus sacked,' Casey said. 'What if Finch and his mother are telling the truth about what time he got home that morning, and it's Clarke who's lying?'

*   *   *

Casey had gone alone to number 5 Railway Road, where the Clarkes now resided with Lily's parents. Gail, for her part, had returned to Finch's house with another officer, to interview him and his mother yet again about when he'd arrived home.

Clarke, unshaven and scruffily dressed,

was home alone when he opened the door to Casey. He was meant to be getting the tea for when they all came in from work, he said. The implication being that Casey had better get on with it. There was little sign of culinary activity in the kitchen, from what she could see, however, apart from a sink full of dirty pots. But she decided to give him the benefit of the doubt.

'So, Lily's got herself another job, then?' she asked.

He looked surprised at the mention of his wife's name. It was clear he was already trying to work out just how much Casey knew about him and his family. She'd picked up a couple of shifts at the pub, he growled, suddenly gripped with domestic fervour. She watched him fill the sink with hot water and squirt it full of bubbles. Rolling up his sleeves, he began attacking the dirty dishes, his back to Casey so she couldn't see his face.

'I know about what Sadie did to her,' she said. 'Nobody would blame you for being angry with her. Did you kill her, Daniel?'

'No.' His denial came out in a squeak and the washing up took on even more fervour.

Why was it, she asked him, that Finch still swore Clarke had driven him straight back to his mum's?

'He's lying,' Clarke said.

Casey's phone beeped a message. Casey read it and smiled.

'That was a message from my colleague,' she said. 'She's at Cameron's house now.'

More clatter from the sink.

'Looks like you've got your facts mixed up, Daniel. Cameron's next-door neighbour saw him being dropped off at 6.30 exactly, from a white van with your registration number.'

'You've checked my registration number?'

'That's what we do, Daniel.'

'He's lying too.'

On the contrary, Casey said. Mrs Finch's neighbour had been leaving the house at the same time — 6.30 — every day for the last fifteen years to go to work.

It suddenly went quiet at the sink.

'We also check to see if the person

we're interested in — you, in this case — has a criminal record.' She paused briefly, before adding, 'You do.'

She reminded him of a fight he'd got into outside a pub a few years back. There'd been a lot of lads involved. Cameron had been one of them.

'So we've got both your DNA and his.'

What was he thinking right now, Casey wondered? It was impossible until she could see his face.

'Do you know what a clinching block is, Daniel?' she said.

'No.'

'Neither did I, until a couple of hours ago,' she said. 'You might not know what it's called. But I bet you'd recognise one if you saw one. In fact, I'm pretty sure you would. It's with forensics at the moment. It belongs to Cameron, so it'll be easy to explain if his DNA's on it. Not so easy to explain the presence of yours, though.'

He turned round at last. There was sweat on his brow; his hands were coated with bubbles that began to drip from his hands onto the kitchen floor.

'I think you picked it up from the floor of the stable when you drove there after you'd dropped Cameron off,' she said. 'And I think you used it on Sadie Warren when you went to have it out with her about what she'd done to your wife.'

Casey reached for a tea towel and threw it towards him. He caught it and cradled it in his hands.

'I bet she laughed at you,' she went on. 'That's when you grabbed the first thing you saw and hit her with it.'

'She deserved it,' Daniel croaked. 'She shouldn't have laughed at me like that.'

Casey heard the front door open, followed by footsteps. When she looked up a young woman — Lily, she presumed — was standing at the kitchen door.

'Dan?' she said. 'What's going on?'

He stood there, dumbstruck, still clutching the tea towel to him like a child with a comforter.

'Are you going to tell her, Daniel?' Casey said. 'Or shall I?'

* * *

154

The evening sun still had some warmth in it as Casey, Dom, Finlay and Oscar the dog strolled along the sea front. Supper at the pub, Dom had said, taking one look at Casey as he opened the door to her. When she was too tired even to look for her keys, he knew that was the right thing to say.

'I'm having burger and chips,' Finlay said, holding onto Oscar's lead as if his very life depended upon it.

'Good choice,' Dom said. 'I might join you. What about you, Casey?'

'What?'

She was miles away and food was the very last thing on her mind. She was still thinking of Lily Clarke's face as uniform arrived to take her husband away.

'What meal?' Finlay jumped in.

The pub was in sight now. They stopped for a while to allow Finlay to untangle the lead from round his ankle. Oscar gazed up at his new master, such trust in his eyes. It was a delight to see them both together, already so fond of each other.

'Fish and chips,' she said, at last.

'Followed by the biggest ice cream in the world.'

The diet would have to wait until tomorrow. Besides, they had a dog now. She'd get plenty of exercise, now Oscar had joined the family.

Deadline News

Joy Hart sat at her computer on the third floor of the offices of The Daily Gazette. Normally this room was full of noise: other journalists exchanging banter or barking down their phones, or those colleagues who constantly mistook their keyboard for a punch bag, all of which made concentrating a real struggle.

But now it was late and everyone had gone home. All she could hear was the traffic outside, the rain pattering against the windows and the combined background thrum of the overhead lighting and computers, a soothing sound that had helped concentrate her mind so wonderfully tonight that she'd been able to wrap up the story she'd been so desperate to finish in record time.

Not the usual trash this time — the gossip and the celebrity scandal she was paid such a vast amount to write, but which, these days, she found so dissatisfying. No, this was something far more important. This was the kind of stuff she should be writing — she hadn't felt so good for ages.

'Take me off this column,' she'd pleaded to Tony so many times. 'Give it to somebody else. Somebody who gives a damn about how many pairs of shoes the latest Hollywood starlet has, or the yo-yo weight of some reality show D-lister.'

But it was like banging your head against a brick wall. As The Gazette's editor, he couldn't lose *Hart to Heart*. It would be professional suicide, he said. It was the stuff their readers wanted to read and, once upon a time, it had been the stuff she'd wanted to write.

Not any more though. These days, what interested her most was getting to the truth. She'd got there, finally, after months of investigation, and now she was ready to show the world. She couldn't wait.

She decided to hang on until the rain eased off. Kill a bit of time getting ahead on her midweek column. She soon became engrossed, her fingers moving swiftly over the keys. She didn't hear the lift gliding smoothly up to the third floor, or the doors opening with a whisper to expel her murderer. She heard his footsteps, soft and dangerous. But by then it was too late. He was far too swift for her. She felt the cord around her throat tighten and pull. She tried to struggle but it was no use. The darkness was already enfolding her.

★　★　★

D.I. Ed Bailey wasn't particularly enamoured of the canteen's full English. The eggs were invariably either under- or overcooked, and the bacon either frazzled to a crisp or so unappealingly limp and anaemic-looking that becoming vegetarian actually began to sound like an attractive option, even for a committed carnivore like himself.

So why had he ordered it then? Stevie, his D.C., would tell him he was comfort eating — making up for Mercy, who didn't seem to want to eat a proper meal at all these days. His own fault that, for letting his guard down one night at The Hope and Anchor after a long and messy day, and confiding his ex-wife's suspicions that their teenage daughter might be anorexic.

He should never have insisted on that third pint. It wasn't as if Stevie was the type to reciprocate. Closed book, was that one. If she had boyfriends, she never mentioned them. All she seemed to be interested in was the job.

'Course, that's what made her such an excellent partner. They'd developed a bond over the three years they'd worked together as a team — a bond based on trust. Ask any copper and they'd know straight off what you were talking about. You had to trust your partner; if you didn't, you'd never pluck up the courage to go out there and put yourself in danger every day, just to do your job.

Stevie could read him like a book. Unsurprising, considering the amount of time they spent together. Not that you'd need to be all that clever to see how he felt about Barker, the new Superintendent. Stevie was with him now, getting on the right side of him, as she'd put it, her chocolate brown eyes flashing accusingly.

'If you were nice to him then he'd be nice to you,' she'd suggested once, when he'd passed some snarky remark about how Barker favoured figures and quotas over people, and wondered if perhaps the man should have become an accountant instead of a police officer.

Barker was a good man, she insisted, despite his faults. He wanted to put the bad guys away just as much as they did. These days, Ed kept the real reason he disliked Barker so much to himself. The fact was, Ed was a man five years off retirement, and set in his ways. And Stevie was a young D.C., keen, ambitious. And ripe for promotion.

Maybe if he made a bit more effort to look younger, he might convince Barker he still had a dynamic future in the force. Lost weight, did something with his hair. A lot of men who were thin on top did that thing where they shaved what little hair they still possessed right off.

But with his blunt features he suspected such a drastic hair cut would make him look as much of a criminal as those he spent his days in pursuit of. He sighed inwardly; there was no hope for him as long as Barker was around.

He'd been so lost in his own thoughts that he'd hardly tasted his breakfast, not even the woolly sausages. But now it seemed his plate was empty. And here was Stevie, back from her little tête-à-tête with the Super, smiling down at him, mug of steaming tea in her hand.

'Mind if I join you?' she said.

He gestured to a chair. He was more than mildly interested to find out what she'd been talking to Barker about, but nothing would have made him ask.

'Though I was just going, actually,' he said. 'I've a report to write. Barker's been on about it for weeks. Looks like this might be a quiet day for a change, so I might as well get on with it.'

'Good,' she said, sitting down. 'That's a relief. I thought I was going to have to do it myself, just to keep Barker off your back. Why he can't ask you himself instead of getting me to do it, I've no idea.'

'So that's what he wanted, was it?'

She grinned. 'I think he's frightened of you,' she said.

Well, it was comforting to know it worked both ways.

'Somehow, he seems to think I can keep you in line better than he ever could,' she added. 'But I had to put him straight. I've worked with Ed Bailey for three years, I told him. I wouldn't work with anyone else. He's a brilliant cop. But he does things his way. So you're wasting your time if you think you can get him to toe the line.'

'You didn't say that did you?'

She smiled enigmatically. 'I said some of it,' she said. 'Up to you to work out which bits.'

He knew he should say something, show his appreciation. But he was too overcome by her loyalty to come up with anything more eloquent than a thank you. As it was, he didn't have time to offer her even that. Out of the corner of his eye, he caught sight of a uniformed officer approaching their table. He was obviously in a big hurry. It looked serious.

'What's up?' he called out, before the P.C. had even reached them.

'Looks like a murder, sir,' the P.C. said. 'At the offices of The Daily Gazette. You both need to get over there.'

★ ★ ★

Less than twelve hours later, Ed stood before his team in the hastily thrown together Investigation Room. As the senior investigation officer, with Stevie by his side, it was his job to inspire the troops. An easy task right now, because at this early stage in the investigation everyone was wide awake and mustard sharp.

Later on, as days dragged into weeks, or weeks dragged into months, officers lost their edge. They grew tired, lazy, sloppy; this was when mistakes were made.

On the board behind him was a plan of the sleek, modern, four-storey building which housed The Daily Gazette. The

166

layout was simple. All the floors, apart from the reception area on the ground floor, were laid out in exactly the same way, each with three conference rooms plus a couple of relaxation areas, all similarly furnished with comfy-looking chairs and low tables. And on each floor there was a large office space lined with serried ranks of computers.

It was in one such space — on the third floor — where the body of Joy Hart had been discovered by a cleaner at around seven that morning. According to Dr Carl Lyle, first to attend as Divisional Surgeon, the cause of death was asphyxia by strangulation. Whoever it was must have come up behind her while she was engrossed in her work. The attack would have been over in seconds.

While he'd been waiting for the doctor to complete his preliminary examination, Ed — who'd been next on the scene along with Stevie, the photographer, and other members of the forensic team — had had plenty of opportunity to work out where all the exits and entrances were, which would stand him in good stead when it came to trying to work out exactly how the murderer had managed to gain access to a place that appeared to be more secure than Fort Knox.

He'd just finished pointing them all out to everyone when the door burst open to reveal Superintendent Barker. Ed felt a rush of irritation. What, in the name of all that was holy, did he want?

It hadn't escaped his notice that on Barker's entrance, the whole room had fallen silent. Everyone was suddenly sitting up straighter too. They didn't do that when he walked into a room. Without acknowledging his entrance, Ed continued to speak, leaving it to Stevie to offer the Super a seat.

'Now,' he said, 'what do we know about Joy Hart? Who would want to take her life? She was single, attractive, a high earner by all accounts. According to colleagues, she kept herself to herself. Worked hard.'

One of the younger officers, Jack Watkins, was desperate to catch his eye.

'What is it, Jack?'

'I interviewed the woman who sits at

the desk behind her, sir,' he said. 'Harriet Shawcross. She writes about finance, she said.' He scrabbled around in his notebook for the relevant information, clearing his throat before he read out her statement. 'In recent months, I noticed Joy was spending more and more time at her desk, arriving before me in the morning and leaving late at night. When I asked her what she was working on she said it was some stuff of her own.' He looked up. 'She seemed to think this was out of the ordinary and worth reporting, sir,' he added.

'Hmm. I see. Perhaps we can get a look at her computer,' Ed said. 'Find out what this stuff of her own was, exactly.'

Stevie frowned.

'The woman may be dead, sir. But she's still entitled to her privacy,' she reminded him. 'You'd need to have evidence there was something relevant to her murder on that computer before they let you anywhere near it.'

Stevie was right, of course. Still, it was an interesting enough scenario to keep in the back of his mind.

'Can I read the rest of Harriet Shawcross's statement, sir?' Clearly, Jack hadn't finished yet.

Ed told him to go on.

'I wondered if it might be an excuse and she wasn't working on anything at all apart from her column, and that the real reason she was spending so long at the office after hours was to meet up with her boyfriend,' he read out.

Ah! A boyfriend.

'Did you get the boyfriend's name?'

Jack looked triumphant. 'Gary Thomas. He works there as a security guard. Harriet Shawcross described him as Joy Hart's bit of rough.'

There was a collective chuckle round the room.

'Anyone spoken to him?'

A second officer raised her hand — Jill Smith, Jack's partner on the job.

'Gary Thomas was on duty all night. Turned up at ten, clocked off at seven this morning.'

'And he didn't see anything?'

'No, said not. Said it was quiet. Went up to see Joy when he got in, but she was short with him. Sent him packing. Said he knew it must look bad, but her manner with him made him angry. They had words. He stormed out. Didn't go back up again for the rest of his shift.'

'Interesting. Do we know anything about him?'

'Just running a check on him now, sir. Must admit, as suspects go, someone with access to all areas is pretty high up on the list. Especially if that someone admits to having had an argument with the victim just prior to her death.'

There was a murmur of agreement. From the corner of his eye, Ed noticed the Super nodding thoughtfully, rubbing his chin between thumb and finger as he did so.

Stevie chimed in, 'When I spoke to the editor, Tony Page, he had a few things to say about Gary Thomas too. Notably, that when Thomas was around, Hart acted differently.'

'In what way?' Ed said.

'Well, Page reckons she was the ballsy type. Would stand no nonsense. But when she was with Thomas she was . . . What was the word he used now?' Stevie wrinkled her brow, searching for the word. 'Submissive, that was it. Also said that Gary Thomas was ex-Army. So he'd presumably have no problems seeing somebody off, would he?'

Ed was just about to make a few more enquiries about Tony Page's interest in the deceased when Barker interrupted him.

'Whatever we do, we've got to wrap this case up ASAP. We can't afford to be seen as being incompetent. The press will make mincemeat of us if we drag it out,' he snapped.

'But if we act too quickly and end up with the wrong man, we'll be even more of a laughing stock,' he said.

But the Super was in no mood to listen to reason. 'Pull him in,' he growled. 'What are you waiting for, Bailey?'

* * *

Going on appearances alone, Gary Thomas had 'possible suspect' stamped all over him. The Super had eyed him up, delight clearly written across his face, as two burly police officers had escorted Thomas to the interview room. He was even more delighted to hear that, when visited at his home by two different burly police officers, Thomas had launched himself at one of them and bloodied the man's nose, putting him on a charge of assaulting a police officer in the line of duty. Further evidence, in the boss's eyes, that Gary Thomas was a wrong 'un.

He was tall, mid-to-late thirties Ed would have said, tattooed to the hilt up both arms, and equipped with the kind of physique that could only have been obtained by spending more hours in the gym than Ed considered healthy.

Thomas sat slumped forward in his seat, his big arms crossed in front of him, resting on the table, all the better to display his tattoos. So far, all Ed had managed to glean from him was that Thomas had been working at The Daily Gazette as a security guard for ten months, that it was in that capacity he'd met Joy Hart, and that their relationship was what he described as 'off and on'.

But getting even such basic information hadn't exactly been easy. Thomas was clearly in no mood to co-operate. During one particularly drawn-out silence, Ed caught Stevie's eye. She nodded imperceptibly. It was their private signal. Time for her to have a go.

'Look, Gary,' she said. 'We just want a chat. It'd be nice if you'd co-operate.'

He glared at her.

'You were in the Army, is that right?'

He nodded. 'Queen's Royal Lancers,' he said.

'When did you leave?'

'Three years ago.'

'Serve in Afghanistan?'

He nodded, looking wary.

'That must have been tough.'

'Look, is any of this relevant?' the brief wanted to know.

Stevie ignored him.

'Gary,' she went on, 'would you say you had a bit of a temper?'

Thomas glanced uneasily at his brief, who looked equally uncomfortable.

'I was provoked when I hit that copper,' he said. 'He asked for it.'

'And are you often provoked?' Stevie's smile ended at her eyes. Ed knew that nothing riled her more than the thought of violence towards women. 'Did Joy Hart ever provoke you, for instance? Did she ask for it?'

Gary Thomas's jaw began to work and he clenched his fists menacingly. Ed decided it was time to step in before somebody else got hurt.

'OK,' he said. 'I'm going to wrap this interview up.'

Stevie gave him a startled look. 'But, sir . . . ' she said.

His phone bleeped. Ed cut her off with a gesture. She was furious, but he'd have to deal with it. It was forensics on the phone. Just to let him know that the rope that had been used to strangle Joy Hart revealed little DNA evidence of any kind. They'd let him know what else they found as soon as they found it. Gary Thomas's solicitor was right. They had no further reason to detain him.

'You're free to go, Mr Thomas,' Ed said.

Thomas drew back his lips in a long,

lingering sneer as he rose from his seat and left the room.

★　★　★

'You let him go?'

Superintendent Barker sat at his desk, drumming his fingers furiously.

'We thought it best,' Ed said.

'*You* thought it best,' Stevie muttered, mutinously.

In the last hour, further information had arrived from the forensic team. Among the prints and DNA found on Joy Hart's desk and chair, some belonged to Gary Thomas.

'Isn't this evidence enough?' Barker said, holding up the print out.

'No,' Ed insisted. 'Look, this is an office. Gary Thomas patrols it, day and night. Not to mention he's probably been there alone with Joy Hart at night when she's been working late — just the two of them, if you know what I mean.'

Stevie rolled her eyes at Ed's coyness. She liked to call a spade a spade.

'We need to wrap this case up,' Barker

said. 'Didn't I tell you that from the get-go?'

'Remember what Tony Page said,' Stevie put in. 'She was different with Thomas. Submissive. Suggests to me she was frightened of him. Perhaps she had a reason to be.'

Ed sighed. 'But this is pure conjecture,' he said. 'And hearsay.'

'The man's an Army veteran,' Barker put in. 'He's killed armed men. He'd certainly know how to creep up on a defenceless woman with her back to him and strangle her to death.'

'No!' Ed had had enough. 'I'm not having this!' He turned to Stevie. 'You fancy him for this murder because you've already decided he's a bullying misogynist based on something Tony Page said. And you,' he said, swinging his gaze over to Barker, 'are determined to nail him for it just so you can fulfil your quotas and to get the press off your back.'

His two adversaries both let out noises of protest.

'But I'm not having it,' he repeated. 'Whoever committed this murder is still out there. That's the person we should be looking for, not Gary Thomas. So if you'll excuse me, that's exactly what I intend to do.'

★ ★ ★

Ed threw himself into his chair, spilling the scalding hot coffee he'd grabbed en route from the Super's office onto his knuckles, and swearing loudly through the pain. Fortunately, there was no one in the office.

Calm down, he told himself. You'll give yourself a heart attack. Far better to concentrate his energy on what to do next, he decided, mopping himself up with a tissue. Maybe he should make a start by re-reading the statements the team had collected.

One in particular beckoned to him. Harriet Shawcross's. Thankfully, Jack had already typed it up and entered it into HOLMES. Two clicks and Ed was into the system. Apart from a few other statements, the file so far was rather thin. Hopefully, forensics would come through with more evidence soon, because Ed, for one, was not content that they'd got their man so easily.

Interesting that Harriet Shawcross had made a point of mentioning how Hart's routine had changed over the last few months. She seemed to be suggesting that it had something to do with Gary Thomas — that the office, when it was deserted, was where they held their rendezvous. Of course, that may well have been the case. But what if she'd been letting her imagination run away with her? The same way Super had, fitting people up because it was convenient.

He scanned the statement once more. Two sentences in particular stood out: 'I noticed she was spending more time at her desk. When I asked her what she was working on, she said it was some stuff of her own she needed to concentrate on.'

How about taking Joy Hart at her word? If she'd said she was working on stuff of her own, then why not believe her? He decided to pay this Harriet Shawcross a visit. What did he have to lose? Anything was better than sitting cooped up here. And at least there'd be no chance of running into the Super in the offices of The Daily Gazette. He was far too busy searching for new ways to fit Gary Thomas up so he could successfully add to this month's targets.

* * *

According to the receptionist — an immaculately made-up young woman whose dark purple nails looked like they could do someone serious damage — Harriet Shawcross was probably some-where on the ground floor having coffee. That's where all the journos were hanging out while the third floor was still a crime scene, apparently. Suddenly, none of them wanted to work from home, she told him. Funny that, she added, dryly.

Never having met Harriet Shawcross before, he only had the receptionist's description to go on. Short hair, no make-up, manly jacket, trousers and flat shoes was what she said. But Ed was convinced she was suggesting a great deal more. She was obviously a person who

180

took pleasure from speaking in code.

He found Shawcross quickly, sitting in a squashy leather chair in a quiet corner, with a cup of black coffee and her laptop for company, checking her Facebook page. Things were clearly quiet in the world of finance today. When he introduced himself, she sat up straight, immediately interested, and gestured to the seat opposite.

'I was just thinking about how a cigarette might put me in the mood to do a bit of work. Now you've turned up, I can put both off a bit longer.'

'Trying to cut down? On the cigarettes, I mean, not on the work.'

'If my girlfriend had her way, there'd be no cigarettes, no coffee and absolutely no fast food of any description,' she said. 'Those fitness fanatics can be hell to live with. So, I heard on the grapevine they arrested Gary Thomas.' Harriet Shawcross fixed her eyes on his. Straight down to business, then.

'He was taken in for questioning, yes. But now he's free.'

Not for long, if the Super has his way,

he neglected to add.

'How serious was Joy Hart's relationship with Thomas?' he said, instead.

She raised an eyebrow. 'Do people still use that dreadful expression, 'toyboy'? You've seen him, Detective. He's hardly the thinking woman's crumpet, is he?'

'From what I've read of them, Joy Hart's columns weren't exactly what you'd call weighty,' he replied.

'Don't underestimate her,' she said. 'Joy had a brain. Did you know she had a first from Oxford?'

He didn't.

'I'm glad you came back, actually,' she said. 'I've been rethinking something I told the officer who interviewed me last time.'

'Oh?'

'I may have given the impression that the beginning of Joy's affair with Gary coincided with the change to her routine.'

'And it didn't?'

'I don't think so, no. Not now I've had time to think properly. Her fling with Gary only started about four months ago. She'd been coming in early and leaving late well before that.'

He wasn't quite sure what she was getting at. But she was a journalist, he reminded himself. A good journalist had hunches just as often as a good detective did.

'I can't help thinking it might be significant. I never saw her as engrossed in the column as she was in this private stuff she said she was doing. More often than not, she'd put the former off as long as she could, and have to be reminded to get on with it. Whatever it was she was writing on the side, it was obviously far more important to her than the day job.'

Ed had arrived at the offices of The Daily Gazette feeling as if the world — in the shape of the Super and Stevie — had joined forces to break his spirit. But when he said his goodbyes to Harriet Shawcross, having left her his card just in case anything else occurred to her that she might think was significant, he was a different man. A man of purpose. Barker was wrong about Gary Thomas, and he was going to take great pleasure in proving it.

First things first, though — and this couldn't wait until he got back to the office — he needed to take a closer look at Joy Hart's computer. Ed took the lift up to the third floor. Luck was with him. Two members of the forensics team, Ann Birch and Geoff Brock, were up there in the office space, fully engrossed in their task of combing the area for anything that might possibly be evidence.

'Come to join us, Inspector?' Ann called out when she realised who it was. 'You'll have to get yourself gowned up first.'

'I need the techies to take a close look at Joy Hart's computer,' he said, taking the gown and gloves from her and removing them from their sterile packaging. 'I want to see what's on it.'

'Did you hear that, Geoff?' Ann called out to her companion. 'The Inspector wants you to remove the hard drive from the victim's computer so the whiz kids can examine the data.'

Geoff nodded from across the room and gave a double thumbs-up sign.

'You've made his day, sir,' Ann said, in

her soft Geordie accent. 'He's never happier than when he's taking things apart. I bet he used to put his poor mother through torture when he was a little boy.'

Ed chuckled, struggling to get the overalls on. It took him so long that by the time he was fully covered, Geoff — who was much more dexterous — had already pretty much dismantled Joy Hart's machine. Ed made his way over to observe him at his work. He knew nothing about the hardware of computers — had never been interested. As long as he could send and receive emails, access HOLMES as and when he needed for information on the cases he was working on, and book his cinema tickets online, then he was satisfied.

Geoff stood over the machine, which was now spread across Joy Hart's desk, turning bits of it over in his hands.

'What's to do?' Ed asked. 'You look puzzled, Geoff.'

'Not so much puzzled,' Geoff said, his voice muffled from behind his mask, 'as intrigued. And so will you be.'

'Why's that then?' Ed asked.

'It's the hard drive,' Geoff said. 'It's not there. Someone's taken it.'

* * *

Ed was more than ready for another confrontation with the Super. His mind worked quickly as he headed back to the office. Why would someone remove the hard drive — the main memory that stored Joy Hart's documents? Was there something on it that someone wanted to keep out of the public domain? And if so, what sort of something?

By the time he reached the station, he was feeling exhilarated. This was what he loved most about his job — the way that events could take such an unexpected turn that even those holding the most hardened preconceptions would have no choice but to relinquish them.

It was in this optimistic frame of mind that he marched into the Super's office without knocking. Barker was at his desk, staring at his computer screen, a smug smile curling his lips. Stevie was leaning over his shoulder, reading something on the screen, her arms folded across her chest, her expression deadly serious. They both looked up, startled, when he entered the room.

Ed began talking before Barker could chastise him for barging in without knocking. It took him only moments to put them in the picture.

'Now you know as much as me,' he said, as he concluded his summary of the events of the morning by revealing the most important piece of information — the missing hard drive.

'I don't see how that's got anything to do with anything,' Barker said. 'Not now we've got this . . . '

There was a gleam in his eye that Ed didn't like the look of. He knows something I don't, he realised. He shifted his gaze to Stevie, waiting for her to shed light on Barker's mysterious pronouncement.

'I know you don't want it to be so, Ed,' she said. 'But we've just had some new evidence in about Gary Thomas. It seems he's got previous for domestic violence.'

Ed stared at her. 'How do you mean?'

This discussion wasn't remotely working out in the way he'd anticipated.

'He put his ex-partner in hospital. In a coma. She had a restraining order against him. He's a nutter.'

'When was this?'

'Does it matter when?' the Super butted in, impatiently. 'Isn't it enough to know that the man is a wife beater? If he can attack one woman so viciously as to put her in a coma, I'd say he's capable of murdering another.'

Ed didn't reply.

'Come on, Ed,' Stevie said. 'You know it makes sense.'

He stood there, waiting for this new information to compute, wishing they weren't both staring at him. He was used to the Super's smugness, but the expression of pity on Stevie's face was something he'd never seen before. He couldn't bear it. It was as if the penny had suddenly magically dropped and she'd seen him for the fool he was.

On the way here he'd been so certain that this case was about to take a new turn. But now what? It looked like, between them, Stevie and the Super had got it all sewn up and he was simply redundant.

Get a grip, he told himself. You're being ridiculous. Remember, you've been here before. From somewhere deep inside he managed to dredge up some of that inner confidence he'd always been able to rely on when he found himself the only person in the room thinking something different from the rest.

He was a good cop. Not just because he said so himself. He'd won a citation once, for goodness' sake. Yvonne hadn't stopped bragging about it to her friends for months. Spent a fortune on a new outfit for the ceremony and made him buy a new suit, even though he had a perfectly adequate one hanging in the wardrobe. This new information was interesting, certainly. But what, fundamentally, did it change?

'What do we know about Gary Thomas?' he began. 'He was a lowly corporal in the Army. A wife beater, it turns out. But there is still no real evidence that he had anything to do with the death of Joy Hart. It's all circumstantial.'

'He put someone in a coma,' Stevie exploded.

'I know that. But don't you see that this new information sheds a very different light on things. Gary Thomas is a security officer. He's no computer geek.'

The Super gave a snort of derision. 'Anyone can remove a hard drive from a computer,' he said.

'Well, I wouldn't know how,' Ed said. 'Would you?'

Silence. Ed decided to take that as a no.

'It just doesn't tie up. OK, so Gary Thomas beats up women. Which makes him a thug and a low life. But not necessarily a murderer. What he did is bad enough, obviously,' he said. 'But I'm saying that there's an alternative scenario. Joy Hart was in possession of some valuable information that had the potential to do great damage to another person or organisation. The person who murdered her knew she had this information.

Maybe he asked her to give it to him. Or to destroy it. Whichever it was, when she wouldn't, he killed her, opened up her computer and removed it himself. Or herself, of course.'

'Now, look here!' The Super interrupted him loudly. 'I've had quite enough of this silliness, D.I. Bailey.'

Silliness! What kind of a word was that? Ed decided to ignore it.

'We've got our man. End of. And I think it would be better all round if you were taken off the case.'

Ed couldn't believe his ears. 'You can't do that!' he said, disbelievingly.

'I can. And I already have,' the Super said, his tone icy. 'Take the weekend off. Come back Monday. And be prepared to forget all about this case from now on. Both of you.'

★ ★ ★

Stevie was outside, smoking, when Ed came through the exit, still furious. He didn't spot her until she spoke to him.

'Thanks, boss,' she said, taking a final

drag before grinding out the stub beneath her heel. Talk about a symbolic gesture.

'I'm sorry,' he said. 'But it's not my fault. Barker's an idiot.'

'So you keep on saying,' she said. 'It's old news. You've set yourself up against him from the off, and now you've gone for the stand-off. And because we're a team, I have to come off the case as well as you. Just when we were getting somewhere, too.'

'We're still getting somewhere, Stevie. I just don't know where yet. But I do know it's not the same destination Rob Barker's got in mind.'

'Yeah, well. It doesn't matter anymore, because come Monday it's got nothing to do with us. I expect Barker'll find a way to punish us by giving us the most boring case imaginable.' Stevie had come outside without a jacket. She hugged herself and stamped her feet against the chill.

'At least we've got the weekend ahead,' she said, after an awkward pause. Perhaps she thought she'd been too harsh with him, Ed thought. 'Doing anything special?'

Ed suddenly froze. Oh no! Yvonne was going to kill him. He groped for his phone. Why hadn't he checked his messages this morning before he left the flat? Three missed calls and three texts, the last one of which was the most frantic.

'Dad. Where are u? I'm at King's X. U were meant to be here 30 mins since. Can't get taxi to ur place cos no money. Pls come and get me ASAP.'

'You okay, boss?' So she did care, after all. At least a little bit.

'Actually, no,' he said. 'If Mercy's rung Yvonne to tell her I've forgotten to meet her, then I'm a dead man.'

★   ★   ★

He found Mercy at the little accessories concession where she'd told him she'd be. She was riffling through a rail of scarves, pausing occasionally to examine one that caught her eye. The last thing Yvonne had said to him on the phone when they'd made this arrangement for Mercy to spend the weekend in London with him was, 'Tell me how you think she looks.'

Was she too skinny? From a distance, wrapped up in several layers, she looked to Ed just like any of the other teenage girls prowling the crowded shop. It was only when he got closer that he noticed how thin her face had become since last he'd seen her, making her eyes, ringed in dark make up, look huger than ever.

'Dad! You muppet!'

It reassured him that her voice was as big and strong as ever. They hugged each other tightly, he repeatedly apologising for being so late and she assuring him that it didn't matter, he was here now and besides she'd had a great time looking at all the stuff in the shop.

'So,' he said, when he finally let her go. 'It's well past dinner time. You must be hungry. I know I am.'

Mercy's expression changed. He'd seen that look on many a suspect's face. She was getting ready to spin him a yarn.

'Actually, I had something on the train,' she said. 'I'm not hungry at all anymore.'

'Never make an issue of food,' Stevie

had said to him, that night in the pub. 'It's the fastest way to escalate the situation if they've already got issues about eating.'

'What did you have?' he said, totally ignoring Stevie's advice.

'Oh, you know. Sandwich, cake, crisps. A fizzy drink. All rubbish.'

'I remember when you could get a proper, decent, hot meal in the buffet car,' he said.

'Good old days, eh, Dad?' Mercy sighed. 'Now it's just pre-packed sandwiches and plastic cups.'

Ed felt sad as they walked out of the station. It looked like his daughter had already grown into a practiced liar. He knew without a shadow of a doubt that there was no buffet bar on the train from Cambridge to King's Cross. Never had been, as far as he knew.

'Dad. Your phone.' Mercy was tugging on his jacket sleeve. They were out on the forecourt now, Mercy hanging onto him for dear life. London terrified her, she'd told him many a time.

He reached for it, but didn't recognise the number. As soon as she spoke, though, he recognised the voice; deep, female, cultured. It was Harriet Shawcross.

'When you gave me your card, you said I could ring if anything else occurred to me.'

Ed stopped walking, forcing Mercy to a standstill. The crowds streamed past them in every direction. He cupped his ear to hear her better.

'What is it, Harriet?' he said.

'I think you should come over to the newspaper offices, as soon as you can,' she said. 'I've just checked my pigeon hole. There was a package in there addressed to me. And a note. It's from Joy. She must have sent it before she was murdered.'

'A package?' he said. 'Have you opened it? What's in it?'

'It looks like the hard drive from her computer,' Harriet said.

'Stay where you are. I'm coming over.'

* * *

Harriet Shawcross was waiting for him on the narrow side street outside the Gazette building.

'I needed a cigarette,' she said, apologetically, holding it up for him to see. 'This has really shaken me up.'

Her gaze flickered briefly over Mercy. 'Is she with you?'

'My daughter. I'm sorry, but I had no choice.'

He felt bad, apologising for his daughter's existence to someone he'd only met on one previous occasion. Thankfully, Mercy was plugged in to her iPod and couldn't have heard.

'No, no. That's fine. Let's go inside.' Harriet leaned her whole weight against the revolving door. 'I locked the package in my desk drawer before I came downstairs. Just in case.'

'Is there somewhere my daughter can sit and wait for me?' Ed asked Harriet once they were inside.

'Sure. Here. On the ground floor. The coffee shop's still open for an hour or so. And she can help herself to a copy of today's paper — there are always masses hanging about. Oh, and there's free WiFi if she gets bored.'

'Perfect.'

It took only a matter of moments to get Mercy settled. Ed handed over a fistful of cash in the vague hope she might be tempted to spend it on something to eat, and reminded her not to go wandering off.

Once they'd reached the third floor, Ed had to walk quickly to keep up with Harriet, who practically sprinted to her desk. Quickly she removed the orange A4 internal mail envelope from her drawer and handed it over.

'We weren't particularly friends, Inspector. I don't know why she sent this stuff to me,' Harriet said.

The note took only a moment to read. *This article is what I've been working on,* it said. *I guess I'm getting up some people's noses, if the phone calls and emails I've had recently are anything to go by. I'd feel this were safer if it were out of my hands until I decide my next move.*
J x

Reading her note set alarm bells ringing in Ed's head. If Joy was getting threatening phone calls and emails because someone didn't like what she'd written, then it didn't take a genius to work out that this someone could have decided to translate words into action.

'Looks bad, doesn't it?' Clearly, Harriet had come to the same conclusion.

'It's certainly food for thought.'

'You can put the hard drive into my laptop,' Harriet said.

Ed stared at her. 'I don't know how,' he said. 'Computers aren't really my thing.'

'Then let me,' she said, snatching it back.

'You know how to do that?' Ed found it impossible to keep the admiration from his voice.

'I also know what goes on beneath a car bonnet and how to put up shelves, Inspector,' she teased.

Ed knew he was blushing. 'I'm sorry,' he said. 'I didn't mean to . . . '

'Forget it. No offence taken. All you have to do is re-connect the cable, put the drive in position and clip it in place. Of course, you need to know which way up it goes,' she replied, good-humouredly.

The whole task took no more than fifteen minutes.

'Right,' she said, once she'd rebooted the computer. 'Let's see what all this is about.'

'How do we know what we're looking for?' Ed said.

'Well, maybe you'll want to trawl through her emails and some of these other files later, in case you think they're relevant,' she said. 'But for now, I'd say let's concentrate on this.'

She clicked on a file entitled 'extra-curricular'. The headline jumped out at them. MODEL BEHAVIOUR — WHO IS TO BLAME FOR THE DAMAGE THESE YOUNG GIRLS ARE DOING TO THEIR BODIES? The strap lines below said, 'Speed doled out to girls as young as 15. Agency denies knowledge. Several girls hospitalised. One says, 'I'll never get my life back.'

The article continued:

In the world of modelling, the name David Quaid Models is synonymous with success. Although it's only been around for five years, DQM has gained a reputation as the go-to agency for young models of a certain type: stick-thin, flat-chested and, to those of us not invested in the what's-hot-and-what's-not dictionary of the fashion world, geekward — the word invented by top London fashion blogger, Dee Urban, to mean a mix of gawky, geeky and awkward.

The feature went on to describe how Joy Hart had evidence to prove that appetite suppressors — amphetamines — were doled out on a regular basis to any young model deemed to be 'too fat' for a shoot or a show.

One of the girls I interviewed is now almost wheelchair-bound; another is a long-stay patient in a hospital ward dedicated to the treatment of severe anorexia. She doubts that she will ever be cured, as the damage to her vital organs is just too great. In other cases, I have evidence that girls have variously suffered damage to their sight, dangerous blood clots and severe shortness of breath that has rendered them housebound for over a year.

'This is dynamite,' Ed said at last, when he'd fully digested what he'd read. 'She's accusing this agency of doping young girls like they were fillies on a race track.'

'I bet Joy wished she'd come up with that one,' Harriet remarked. 'If you ever give up the day job, Inspector, you could always try for a career as a journalist.'

'There's more,' Ed said. 'This statement from DQM blames the girls. Says it's common knowledge that this stuff can be bought off the internet, and it's got nothing to do with them.'

'They would, wouldn't they?' Harriet said.

There was a sudden commotion behind them. They both spun round to see Mercy limping towards them, looking as pale as death. She was being held upright by one of the porters who'd greeted them on their way in. Ed leaped to his feet.

'I'm all right,' she said. 'I slipped, that's all. I've twisted my ankle but I haven't broken anything.'

Ed rushed forwards, carefully helping her to a seat. Meanwhile, Harriet grabbed another chair for Mercy to rest her injured foot on.

'She was running up and down the stairs,' the doorman said. 'I asked why and she said she needed the exercise. I lost count how many times. Maybe I should have stopped her. But we don't have no rules about that. So I let her carry on. Until she tripped coming down.'

Harriet was examining Mercy's foot and ankle, pressing each area gently and quietly asking if it hurt. Mercy responded with the odd shake of her head, a nod or the occasional wince.

'Try and stand on it,' Ed said. 'That way we'll know whether to take you to A&E or not.'

'I'm not going to hospital, Dad. It's fine. I just felt a bit dizzy, that's all.' Mercy struggled to her feet. 'Look. There's nothing wrong with my foot. Or my ankle.'

There didn't appear to be. But Ed was still concerned. What could she have meant by needing the exercise? A skinny little thing like her. Quickly, he thanked the doorman, reassuring him that what had happened to Mercy was absolutely not his fault. As soon as he'd departed and the three of them were alone, he let rip.

What did she mean, she felt a bit dizzy? he demanded to know. Did this happen often? And when was the last time she'd eaten something?

'Be honest with me, Mercy,' he pleaded.

'On the train,' she said, her voice small and high. 'Like I told you.'

'That's a lie,' he said. 'There is no buffet car on the Cambridge train.'

Mercy's eyes began to well up with tears and her cheeks grew red. Harriet was by her side immediately, a protective arm around her shoulder.

'I'm not sure this is helping,' she said with a frown.

He wanted to tell Harriet to butt out. This was his daughter, and she was his problem. But it wasn't Harriet he was angry with, as much as himself. One weekend. Two short days. And he couldn't even get that right. Yvonne was right. He was completely rubbish as a parent.

What was he supposed to do now? It was obvious that Mercy needed watching 24/7 — not just to make sure she was eating, but so that no further accidents befell her. He felt torn in two. Joy Hart's note was as disturbing as the article she'd written. She had clearly strongly believed she was being threatened, or she would never have removed that hard drive and sent it to Harriet for safekeeping. But he couldn't just ignore Mercy's problems. He needed to sit down and talk to Yvonne about their daughter, and work out what they were going to do for her.

'I think it would be best if I drove you back home to your mum's, Mercy,' he said.

'What? No! You promised me a film at least,' Mercy protested.

'No.' He was putting his foot down. 'I'm going to ring Mum, then we're going back to my flat, getting in the car and driving to Cambridge.'

There was another phone call he needed to make first, though. He couldn't afford the time to trawl through every single email in Joy Hart's account or check her other files. But Stevie would help him out. She was his partner, wasn't she?

★　★　★

Ed stared out of the lounge window of the house he used to share with Yvonne and Mercy. He had a headache and his bones were screaming after a night spent on the settee.

'If I'd had a bit more warning I'd have made up the spare bed, but these days it's impossible to get to, with all the junk we keep in that room,' Yvonne had told him over the phone when he'd announced he was bringing Mercy back home. He didn't blame Yvonne for her lack of hospitality. She didn't get much time alone and must have been looking forward to having the place to herself this weekend.

On the journey to Cambridge he'd resigned himself to expect the usual accusations of neglect and indifference. But Yvonne had taken one look at Mercy and, ignoring him, fallen upon her, hugging her so tightly and for so long that it seemed to Ed she might smother the girl. Both Yvonne and Mercy had started sobbing uncontrollably, while Ed had stood there awkwardly looking on, not knowing what he could do to make things better.

In the end he'd gone off to the kitchen and made tea for everyone. The simple mechanics of the task took the heat out his emotions. He was going to have to approach this situation calmly and practically, he'd decided. His daughter needed help and he'd get it for her, whatever it cost.

Before leaving for Cambridge, he'd phoned Stevie and asked if he could drop something off at her place because he had a bit of a family emergency and couldn't deal with the problem himself. When he'd told her what it was, and explained how she could help him with it, she'd almost blown a fuse.

Had he forgotten they were both off the case, she reminded him. If it got back to the Super that they'd disobeyed his instructions to keep well away from anything that concerned Joy Hart's murder, then she could kiss goodbye to any chance of promotion, and he might as well put in for early retirement before he got the sack anyway.

'What is this family emergency, anyway?' she'd asked him, once she got to the end of her rant. When he told her about Mercy, her whole attitude softened.

'Drop it off,' she'd said. 'Leave it to me. You do what you've got to do. I'll ring you when there's something to say.'

Yvonne and he had spoken long into the night, putting aside their differences in their mutual concern for their daughter. Today was the day to get things moving. Yvonne had been on the phone most of the morning, and he'd spent most of it online, checking out places that specialised in the treatment of eating disorders. Yvonne had told him that she'd found one that came highly recommended, up north. But he wouldn't be able to give up work any time soon because a place like this didn't come on the NHS, she'd told him, ruefully. Like money mattered at a time like this, he'd replied.

As if the idea of work had triggered a psychic connection to Stevie, his phone rang.

'Boss,' she said, her voice low and urgent.

'Stevie.'

'How's things?'

'Oh, you know. We're getting there. What have you got?'

'What have I not,' she replied. 'Those girls Joy Hart wouldn't identify. We have their names and addresses through her emails. One of them lives in a place called Shelford. That's near you, isn't it?'

'Yes.'

'You need to talk to her. Get her story. She took a lot of persuading to open up to Joy. Said she'd been threatened. If her name, or any pictures of her appeared in print, she was scared of what would happen to her family.'

'Who threatened her? Someone from DQM?'

'The top man — David Quaid himself.'

'I see.'

'It gets better. There's a sound file on Joy's hard drive. A phone call she must have recorded with Quaid. She tells him what she's found out and that she's coming for him. He tells her to back off.

She says she won't. He says she'd better, or else she was going to have to watch her back.'

'That's intimidation,' Ed said. 'I need to know what he meant by that remark.'

'You can't go in there all guns blazing, boss. Not with the Super on your back,' Stevie said. 'Besides, you've only got Joy Hart's word against his. We need to corroborate those girls' statements.'

Stevie was right.

'I'll go to Shelford,' he said. 'I'm only kicking my heels here anyway.'

'Good. And I'll get onto the other girls; they're Home Counties based.'

'Have you said anything to the Super yet?' Ed said.

There was a pause before Stevie said, 'Are you mad?'

'You're a pal, Stevie,' he said.

'Well, if we're going down, we'll be going down together,' she replied.

* * *

'Kelly is staying with her boyfriend up in Scotland,' Mrs Townsend said, showing

Ed into their tiny front room, off the Shelford Road.

It was stuffed to the gills with furniture designed for much more stately quarters — there was a drinks cabinet, an expensive leather suite and the largest plasma screen TV Ed had ever seen — presumably part of the spoils of Kelly's modelling career.

'Scotland?'

He hadn't thought for a minute she wouldn't be at home with her parents. According to Joy Hart's report, the girl had dropped below six stone at one point, and had broken down in tears when interviewed, confessing her fears that she'd never be cured, either of her anorexia or of her addiction to the tablets she'd swallowed like sweeties to enable her to stay on DQM's books.

'That's right.'

He hadn't noticed the husband before, hidden in the folds of one of the leather chairs. The man got slowly to his feet, sending a warning glance to his wife. What was going on here, Ed wondered.

'It's a long way to go,' he said. 'The boy

must be worth it. Perhaps you could give me her address.'

That glance again.

'I'm sure you're relieved that she's recovered enough to live a normal life again,' he added. 'You must have wondered if that day would ever come again.'

He fixed his gaze on Mrs Townsend, willing her to break and tell him where their daughter really was, but she refused to meet his eyes, fixing them firmly on the floor instead.

'I have a daughter, Mrs Townsend,' he said. 'She's just turned sixteen. Turns out she's got an eating disorder. They say it's the bright girls that this dreadful disease afflicts most often, don't they?'

Silence. He plodded on.

'It's a terrible thing when your daughter's in the grip of an illness like this,' he said. 'As a parent, you'd do anything to help them. Anything. Because you blame yourself, don't you? Even though, logically, you know they've been influenced just as much by other things. Other people.'

Finally, Mrs Townsend raised her eyes from the ground and met his gaze. She looked wretched, Ed thought.

'My daughter wasn't well, Inspector,' Mr Townsend said. 'She did some stupid things. Took drugs. Then, when that journalist came round, she tried to blame it on those that had given her all that modelling work. Now she's sorry, and wants to start over again, somewhere new.'

'Mr Townsend,' Ed began to explain, 'I am dealing with some very serious allegations about this particular agency. I can see how you might want to protect your daughter from any unnecessary exposure. But lying to the police is not the best way to protect your child.'

'I'm not lying,' insisted Mr Townsend. 'It was that journalist. Putting nonsense into young girls' heads. Offering them money for a story. Stands to reason they'll say what you want to hear.'

Mr Townsend was clearly agitated.

'Calm down, Mike.' Mrs Townsend rested her arm on her husband's shoulder but he shook it off.

'I think you'd better go, Inspector,' she

said. 'I'll see you out.'

They were well within their rights to show him the door. They'd committed no crime as far as he could tell. But if they thought he could be hoodwinked so easily, they had another think coming. They were keeping something from him, for sure.

'I'll bid you good day,' he said, following his reluctant hostess out.

'I apologise for my husband's temper, Inspector,' Mrs Townsend said, at the door. 'It was a bad time for us all, that. He just wants to put it behind him.'

'I quite understand.'

'Just one thing. The man they arrested for killing that journalist. They've got the right one, haven't they?'

'My boss assures me they do,' Ed said.

Something like relief flickered over Mrs Townsend's face. Why, he wondered. Had she been burdened with misgivings, just like him?

'Are you sure you won't tell me where your daughter's staying, Mrs Townsend?'

She swallowed hard; her eyes were glassy with tears she refused to shed.

'No, I can't,' she said. 'Please. Don't ask me. It's enough she's safe. Now, just go.'

Ed made his way down the garden path and climbed into his car. What now? He was bone-weary. Force of habit made him check his phone. Yvonne, Stevie, Harriet Shawcross, Mercy, and a couple of numbers he didn't recognise. He slipped his mobile back into his pocket and laid his head on the steering wheel. He was only going to close his eyes for a couple of minutes, that was all. Otherwise he'd be in no fit state to drive back to London.

He was startled awake by a tap-tap-tapping on the window. He struggled to open his eyes. When he did, he saw Mrs Townsend staring in at him. She gestured for him to wind down the window, which he did, still befuddled by sleep.

'He's gone for a lie down,' she said. 'My husband suffers from anxiety, and you coming to see us like that and raking everything up again — well, it's a bit too much for him.'

What did she want, he wondered. And how long had he been asleep?

'I waited half an hour until I could be sure he'd dropped off. I saw you hadn't driven away. I kept thinking you would. I told myself, I'll give him ten minutes and if he's still there I'll go outside and give it to him.'

She was holding something out — a small white contact card.

'But I couldn't bring myself to, so I let another ten minutes pass, and then another. So, anyway, here. I've done it now.'

He took the card from her and scanned the contents.

'It's where she's staying. Not with her boyfriend, but you guessed that straightaway, didn't you?' she said. 'It's a private hospital. All expenses paid. As long as we keep our mouths shut. But I can't any more, Inspector. She's my daughter and I love her, and I don't care what happens to me for telling. This man can't be allowed to ruin any more young lives.'

★ ★ ★

Ed's phone rang just as he was fastening his seat belt. It was Stevie and she told a familiar tale. She'd only been able to make contact with a couple of the girls Joy Hart had interviewed, and each one had backtracked, as had their families. It was beginning to feel like a conspiracy of silence, she said.

Ed did his best to cheer her up, quickly filling her in on his conversation with Kelly Townsend's mother.

'It's not so bad,' he said. 'We can get him for supplying, and for intimidation, if she keeps her word and provides us with a statement.'

'But we still have no proof that he's a murderer,' Stevie said.

'So you do believe me that the wrong man's been locked up, then?'

Stevie sighed. 'You're going to make me say I was wrong, aren't you?' she said.

Ed chuckled.

'Okay. I'm sorry I ever doubted you,' she said.

'Apology accepted.'

'Now, enough grovelling. What do we do next?'

'We keep digging,' Ed said.

'Not so easy,' Stevie replied. 'We're not

meant to be on the case, remember?'

Ed's phone bleeped. 'Look, I've got to go. I've got another call waiting. Do what you can, Stevie.'

'Will do,' Stevie said. 'But don't hold your breath.' Then she was gone.

It was Harriet Shawcross on the line. She sounded distraught. 'It's Tony,' she said. 'He's gone missing. And I think it's my fault.'

'What do you mean?'

'I showed him Joy's article. Told him her suspicions.'

'How could you have shown it him?' Ed said. 'The hard drive's with my D.C.'

There was a pause. 'I'm sorry. I took a copy. Force of habit. And I thought Tony should know. He's the editor after all.'

'Never mind all that,' he said. 'What do you mean, Tony's gone missing?'

'He said it needed a diplomatic touch,' she went on. 'That's Tony all over. Don't ruffle feathers, unless it's those of your own journalists. He's terrified of lawsuits.'

'You think he phoned David Quaid?'

'That's what he said he was going to do. They needed to smooth things out, was what he said. Man to man. I left him to it. Went home. When I turned up this morning, everyone else was there, waiting for him in the conference room. But he never showed.'

'Have you tried to ring him? Been round to his house?'

'His phone's switched off. I have his address but, to be honest, Inspector, I'm reluctant to go round there. I keep thinking of Joy. And I'm afraid of what I might find.'

'Text me his address,' Ed said. 'I'm on my way.'

⋆   ⋆   ⋆

The nap at the wheel of his car had refreshed Ed. As soon as he got onto the M11 he kept to the fast lane. In no time, at all he was in Highgate, where Tony Page lived. He pulled up outside the house, which was situated down a quiet side street and strode up to the front door of Page's Edwardian semi.

He rang the bell once, twice, three times. No sound of answering footsteps.

He stood there waiting, a creeping feeling of anxiety spreading over him. Minutes ticked by, but still nothing. All he could make out when he peered through the windows was the outline of the furniture and a few shadowy pictures on the wall.

He decided to try the back way, the access to which was through a tall side gate. Locked, no matter how many times he rattled it. He was just mulling over what to do next, when he heard someone clearing their throat behind him.

Spinning round, Ed found himself confronted by a petite, white-haired, elderly lady grasping a rather lethal-looking garden fork. From the steely determination in her eyes, it was clear she would have no qualms about using it. Immediately he reached for his I.D.

'Oh, dear,' the woman said, once she'd understood its significance. 'Has there been an accident? I did tell him before he set off that I really didn't think he should be driving. He didn't look at all well. I'm Margaret Stewart, by the way,' she added, transferring the garden fork from her right hand to her left, and holding out the former for Ed to shake, which he did, awkwardly.

'You've seen him today?'

'No. Last night. Just before he drove off. Said he was going away for a few days. I rather got the impression that he wished I hadn't seen him. It was quite late and the street was deserted apart from the two of us. He couldn't have expected anyone else to be out at that time of night. We're very quiet round these parts.'

'What time was it?'

'Well past midnight. I was coming back from feeding another neighbour's cat, you see. I should have fed it earlier but I'd been watching an episode of *Vera* I'd recorded and couldn't tear myself away.'

'Did he say where he was going?'

She shook her head. 'No. Like I said. He didn't seem to be in the mood to give anything away. But I think I can guess. He has a cottage down in Suffolk. His little refuge, he calls it. I have the details, if you can just hang on while I look for them. I stayed there once, you see, when I was having my new kitchen fitted and it became impossible to manage, what with . . . '

'That'll be great, Mrs Stewart,' Ed said, firmly interrupting her.

'You might as well come inside while I look for it. It could take a while.'

Ed had had a great many dealings with little old ladies in his time as a police officer. He had no doubts at all that Mrs Stewart would spin out her hunt for at least as long as it took to sit and drink a cup of tea and tell Ed her life story. But if that was what it took, then so be it. He needed to get to Tony Page before David Quaid did, and inflicted the same treatment on him as he had on Joy Hart.

★   ★   ★

Tony Page had been propping up the bar of The Red Lion, staring into an empty pint pot, when serendipity intervened. Ed, exhausted after the long drive to the Suffolk coast, made his way into the pub, drawn inside by the promise of home-cooked, fresh, line-caught fish and chips at a reasonable price, as chalked up on a board by the entrance.

It was only as he'd arrived in the little seaside town that Ed realised he had no idea what to do next if Tony Page wasn't at home, or if he wouldn't open the door to him. But suddenly, there he was, just as if their meeting was meant to be. He'd recognised Page immediately, thanks to the photograph Mrs Stewart had shown him of the street party they'd had the previous summer for the Queen's Diamond Jubilee. He'd looked out of place then, self-conscious and rather formally dressed compared to the neighbours, and he looked out of place now, very much the townie in his suit and tie, among the casually dressed locals with their weather-beaten faces and Suffolk accents.

'How did you find me?'

Ed had persuaded Page to move to a corner table with the incentive of another pint. He noted how the man's hand shook as he lifted the glass to his lips, tipping back his head and sinking a third of its contents in one swallow. Ed told him.

'I might have guessed.' Page replaced the glass on the beer mat. 'She's a one-woman Neighbourhood Watch, is that one.'

'Who are you running away from, Tony?'

'I've no idea what you mean.'

'Oh, come on. Quit stalling. You've read Joy's article. It's obvious who killed her.'

'Why don't you go after him, then?'

'Because I have no real proof. Just a threatening email. It wouldn't stand up in court,' Ed said. 'The most I might be able to charge him with is for the initial crime Joy accused him of.'

Tony Page stared into his glass, like someone hypnotised.

'I think he's threatened you, too, Tony,' Ed said. 'And that's why you've come down here.'

'Yes. You're right. The man's crazy. He threatened to kill me if I went to the police.'

Finally!

'And are you prepared to make a statement to that effect?'

Tony gripped his glass with both hands.

'Yes. I am. I ran away because I'm a coward.' He raised his eyes at last. 'Unlike

Joy. She stood up to him. I owe it to her, because it's my fault she's dead,' he said.

'How?'

'Because the paper didn't back her. I didn't back her. Don't you see? I could have made it a campaign. Splashed it all over the front page. But I told her she should stick to what she knew. Let the broadsheets do the investigative journalism.' He took another long drink. 'If I'd done my job, and taken the lead like a proper editor, she wouldn't have needed to go undercover and put herself in danger. She paid for my cowardice with her life.'

Ed almost felt sorry for him. Journalists didn't have consciences, so common opinion went. But this man clearly did. His sympathy for Page was short-lived, however. A man with a conscience would have supported his staff and done all he could to join Hart in her campaign, not told her to forget it.

'I'm going after him,' Ed said. 'Now. Right away.'

'Cod, chips and mushy peas?'

A smiley-faced young waitress was

looking down at him, holding out a plate of steaming food.

'Give it to my friend here,' Ed said. 'I've just remembered there's somewhere I have to be.'

$$\star \quad \star \quad \star$$

By the time Ed got back to London it was one in the morning. Something had brought him to his senses around about half an hour into his journey. He was far too old for this caper. What had he been thinking, rushing off like that to go after David Quaid? He hadn't even got the man's address!

Even more inexplicable was giving away his fish and chip supper when he hadn't eaten since breakfast. He was an idiot. An exhausted, hungry idiot. It would have to wait until tomorrow. Right now he needed his bed. It was only as he climbed under the duvet that he remembered he'd broken his promise to ring Yvonne and find out how things were progressing with finding help for Mercy. A double idiot, then.

A hammering on the door roused Ed from a deep slumber. He was surprised to see daylight creeping in through the bedroom curtains. Whatever time was it? The bedside clock said six-thirty.

Ed groaned and groped for his dressing gown, struggling to keep his eyes open. Whoever it was clearly wouldn't go away until he answered.

It was Stevie. 'I've been trying to cover for you with the Super,' she said, eyeing him up and down, critically. 'He's furious with you for going off and not telling him what you're up to. We're wanted on another case. You'll love it. Not. License fraud.'

'I've got a case, remember,' he said, opening the door to admit her. 'You'll have to cover for me a bit longer.'

She followed him into the kitchen.

'Actually, while you're here, can you do me a favour while I jump in the shower?' he asked.

'Mop the floor?'

Ed rolled his eyes. 'Get an address for me. David Quaid. I'm planning a little visit. If I get a move on, I should be able to get to him before he leaves for the office.'

'Anything else?'

He was at the door before he thought of what else she could do. 'Pay a visit to his office. Have a look around. There must be something there with his DNA on it.'

'You don't ask for much, do you, boss?' Stevie said, with a wry smile.

★   ★   ★

Quaid lived in Brixton — right at the other end of town to him. He hadn't banked on the traffic and the road works when he'd decided to make this little trip south of the river.

By the time he reached the modern high-rise where Quaid's flat was located, he'd been driving for at least an hour. He was dimly aware of his phone going off several times during the journey but chose to ignore it. He needed all his concentration for the road.

He pulled up on the opposite side of the road to the block of flats. Quaid lived on the seventh floor. Flat number 708. Ed's instinct was to take the man by surprise. But how could he get in and up to his door without giving him prior warning?

When he saw a van draw up outside bearing the words J & T Custom Clean, it was the answer to his prayer. He nipped over the road as the van disgorged half a dozen women of all ages and sizes, each one carrying a plastic bucket containing their cleaning wares, and chatting away merrily. All it took was a friendly smile and a bit of banter and he was inside the building.

The lift brought him up to the seventh floor in no time. Just as he stepped out, his phone pinged again.

'Not now,' he muttered, switching it off. Quaid's door was just opposite. Now that he was here, standing outside it, it occurred to him that perhaps he should have come with back up. Quaid had killed once. He'd threatened to kill Tony Page. If he knew how close Ed was to revealing the truth, how would he react?

Keep calm, he told himself as he rang

the bell. Make him believe you're just here for a friendly chat. Footsteps. The sound of a bolt being slid across the door. A chain being dismantled. Then the door was flung open to reveal a man in his forties, tall, slim, and elegant in his Savile Row shirt and well-cut trousers. The glance he offered Ed, dressed as usual in his shabby overcoat, was a disdainful one.

Ed flashed his I.D. 'I'd like a word,' he said. He was inside before Quaid could even read it.

'What's this about?'

'Joy Hart.'

A shadow passed over Quaid's face. 'Excuse me a minute,' he said. 'I've left the radio on in the bedroom.'

He was out of the room in a flash. Ed remained standing in the middle of the room, examining his pristine surroundings. Maybe he should think about getting a cleaner, he mused, as he waited. It would certainly make his life a lot easier. Quaid was back in no time.

'Have a seat, Inspector.' Quaid gestured to a leather chair.

Ed shook his head. His concentration

may have slipped for a moment, but now he was back on his guard.

'Well, if you won't, I will.' Quaid threw himself down on the matching black leather settee, spread his arms along its back and smiled up at Ed, showing his expensively whitened teeth.

'What was that name again?' he asked.

Ed repeated it. 'Joy Hart,' he said.

Quaid wrinkled his brow. 'Is she one of our models? You might be better off enquiring at the agency. I really can't be expected to remember every single . . . '

Ed had had enough. He'd met men like Quaid before. And every last one of them had always managed to get right under his skin. Casting aside the advice he'd given himself to keep things friendly, he burst out, 'Stop playing games. I know you killed her. She threatened to expose what you were doing — doling out illegal slimming pills to models as young as fifteen. Causing them all sorts of health problems, not to mention getting them addicted.'

'That's nonsense.'

'No. It's the truth. We have it on her

hard drive. Joy Hart's article, with names of the girls you peddled your tablets to. Her emails with the girls' addresses on. Most significantly, we have a recording of the conversation you had with her, telling her to mind her back. You couldn't let her get away with it, and so you visited her at her place of work, came up behind her and strangled her.'

Quaid's brow darkened. The toothsome smile had disappeared. Now his mouth was a thin line. There was something else different too, Ed realised. But what exactly? He racked his brains. That was it! When Quaid had left the room earlier, he hadn't been wearing a jacket. But when he'd returned, he had. And now he was groping in his pocket for something.

A gun. At first, Ed couldn't believe what he was seeing. The man was going to shoot him! No one had ever pointed a gun at him before, in all his time in the police force.

A sense of calm fell over him; he felt no fear. In fact, it all seemed inevitable that he should get to the end of his service with nothing more than the odd scratch and then this. He just wished he could be sure that Mercy would be alright. And he still hadn't called Yvonne, and now she'd think he'd never really cared.

'Police! Get down!'

There was a series of crashes as the door caved in, and three armed officers burst into the room. Ed thought his heart would come leaping out of his chest at the shock of their dramatic entrance.

Quaid was even more taken aback, kicking his weapon away before throwing himself to the ground, exactly as he'd been instructed. And now, here was Stevie, rushing forward to slap the cuffs on Quaid and reading him his rights. Murder. She was charging him with murder as well as for supplying. This must mean that she'd managed to retrieve something useful from his office, and that forensics had found a match.

'You didn't get my messages, then, boss?' she said, when Quaid had been taken away.

Ed, still in shock, could only shake his head.

'He's a member of a firearms club,' she

233

said. 'He has a gun. That was what I said when I rang you. But then, I guess you found that out for yourself, didn't you?'

'I guess I did,' Ed said, ruefully. 'You came up with something at his office, then?'

Stevie grinned. 'Cigarette tips. He has quite a habit.'

★ ★ ★

Ed stood with his hand poised to open the door to the private room where Mercy had been staying for a month now. It had been hard at first. Yvonne was on the phone to him almost every night, crying. The regime was too strict, she said. Mercy hated it and kept asking when she could come home.

He tried to be strong for her. For both of them. 'The doctors told us it wouldn't be easy,' he'd said. 'But if this is going to work then we've got to trust them.' Every night when he put the phone down, he felt dreadful. Mercy was his little girl too.

'Dad!' Mercy must have been listening out for him, because here she was at the door, pulling him inside.

She looked well. There was colour in her cheeks again. She was still thin. But perhaps not quite as painfully.

'Mum says you've got that man for murdering the journalist,' she said, proudly. 'I've been telling all the doctors it was you who got him.'

'Strictly speaking, it was team work,' he said. 'It's always team work in my job.'

Which was exactly what the Super had said to the press when he'd been interviewed about the successful arrest of David Quaid. Funny that, considering how little he'd had to do with the whole thing. Would he still be so cheerful when Gary Thomas slapped a case of wrongful arrest on him, Ed mused.

'You're too modest, Dad,' Mercy said.

She patted the bed and Ed sat down. 'Anyway,' he said. 'Enough about me. How are you? You look so much better than when I last saw you.'

'I've put on four pounds in a month,' she said. 'And from tomorrow I can start choosing my own food.'

This was good news. As good as any

he'd had in a long time. He was lucky. He'd got his daughter back. Some of the parents of those poor girls Joy Hart had been fighting for might have a longer wait.

But Joy's endeavours hadn't been in vain. The Daily Gazette's campaign was making thousands and all of it would go towards their treatment. A trashy gossip columnist? No one would ever think of Joy Hart that way again.

Other titles in the
Linford Mystery Library:

THE HUNTSMAN

Gerald Verner

Superintendent Budd is faced with one of his toughest assignments in separating the strands of mystery that grip the village of Chalebury: a series of robberies perpetrated by the burglar known as Stocking-foot; sightings of the ghostly Huntsman; and the murders of a villager and a local police inspector. Interweaving with these is the suspicious behaviour of a frightened young woman who lives in a large dilapidated house with one elderly servant. Is there a connection between all these crimes and other oddities happening in the tiny village?

DREAMS IN THE NIGHT

Norman Firth

Tiring of her repressed life on a country farm, teenage beauty Alice Graham runs away from home, hoping to find a job as a journalist in New York in the Roaring Twenties. When her money runs out and she is on the edge of despair, she is befriended by Maddie, a veteran of the burlesque theatre, who takes her under her wing. But Alice soon attracts the unwelcome attentions of a New York gangster, which begins a chain of events that ignites a powder keg of murder and ultimate tragedy . . .

DEATH STALKS A LADY

Shelley Smith

After the death of her father, Judith Allen travels across the Atlantic to join the rest of her estranged family in the UK. Upon arrival, she discovers a dead woman in the garage of her mother's house, and is soon thrown into a whirlwind of adventure. As she tries to turn to her family for comfort, the people close to her start dropping like flies in mysterious circumstances. Judith is determined to follow the clues and unmask a murderer. But who can she trust?

A CORNISH BETRAYAL

Rena George

When Loveday inherits the ruins of a remote clifftop cottage, her delight is marred by the mysterious disappearance of a young man from his narrowboat on a Cornish creek. Since he's a chum of her friends, Keri and Ben, she naturally wants to help. But things quickly escalate into a far more serious affair, and it seems her involvement could be doing more harm than good. Despite Loveday's best intentions to steer clear of her detective boyfriend Sam's investigation, she becomes inextricably involved — risking her life in the process . . .

MOUNTAIN GOLD

Denis Hughes

Rex Brandon, internationally famous geologist, is flying to join a party of prospectors camped overlooking the frozen surface of Great Bear Lake in northern Canada, when his plane is forced down in a storm. Suddenly Brandon faces a 200-mile trek across the frozen wastes. Of the people he meets on his journey — all of whom want to get to Great Bear — several are destined to die, and Brandon cannot be certain that the survivors are who they say they are, or what their true motives may be . . .